The Coloured Bangles

and other stories

By Saloni Narang

Three Continents Press

©1984 Saloni Narang

First American Edition
Three Continents Press
1346 Connecticut Avenue, N.W.
Washington, D.C. 20036

ISBN 0-89410-403-9
ISBN 0-89410-404-7 (paperback)
Library of Congress No. 83-50208

Second Edition, revised and augmented
New Delhi © 1984 Saloni Narang

All rights reserved. No part of this book may be used or reproduced in any manner whatsoever, without written permission, except in the case of brief quotations in critical articles and reviews. For information, write the publisher.

Cover Art by Marek Wilczynski

The Coloured Bangles

and other stories

*I just sat in the shadows
and listened to them talk . . .*

from "The Patriot"

Preface

Any effort, however limited, to sketch the world of an Indian storyteller is going to lead to images in contrast, in searing conflict, a kaleidoscope of overlapping time frames, an essay in co-existence. For India is a country of contrasts, of seeming contradictions, where volatile emotions see-saw against a phlegmatic acceptance of the writ of fate; where the sublime philosophy of "Aham Brahmasmi" (I am Brahman, the One Absolute, the Creator and the Created) co-exists with the daily worship of the many-armed, smiling-faced pantheon of mythological gods; where the latest in computor technology rides with perfect non-chalance on the back of an unchanged 3,000 year old model of a bullock cart. A country living simultaneously in many centuries, accepting much, rejecting nothing.

And from this wealth of cultural interplays comes the mind of an Indian storyteller.

When I wrote these stories, I had not intended them to be so diverse in themes, in styles, in settings. The themes, the settings, had to differ greatly one from the other. They were the inevitable growth out of the stimulus which is India. The changing styles merely reflect my joy in the versatility of the English language, a delight in word patterns as they cleave together, sometimes lyrical, sometimes staccato, to blend, to counterpoint, to underline the mood of each story.

Though these stories pick up echoes only from the Northern half of India, this the Northern half which colours my imagination, is a varied canvas, and my backdrops shift from the Westernized sitting rooms of the educated elite to the thatch atop the mud huts of rural India; from an anglicized manager of a West Bengal tea estate face to face with the stark horror of Naxalite* terrorism to the emotional volatility of pastoral Punjab.

Some of the tales included are based on true stories. Among

these are "The Resurrection," "Close to the Earth," "Masterji," "Tea Leaves," and "Uma." The characters are all fictional. Sometimes it is an incident heard which sparks off a story, sometimes a story weaves itself around a setting, as in "The Return." In my mind's eye, I can see the village which still exists and grows "like a wart from a cleft in the lake" and the line of bullock carts still winds its way to and from the sugar factory.

All the stories except "The Coloured Bangles," written in 1983, were composed a decade ago. After some ten years I find I can "afford" to let them live again for new readers.

I would like to thank my most valuable critic, my husband, who always unerringly pinpointed the one missing addition needed to spark the stories to life. Without his encouragement these stories would never have been written. I also thank my publisher for all the time and care he lavished on this little book.

Saloni Narang
Delhi May 1983

---

*An extreme Communist movement centered in the West Bengal town of Naxalbari, most powerful in the 1950's. Thousands of members of the group were killed and others imprisoned after violent protests.

saloni narang

the coloured bangles and other stories

Contents

Author's Preface   vii

The Return	5
Uma	11
The Wolf at the Door	23
Masterji	31
The Resurrection	35
Tea Leaves	41
A Slit in the Fabric	51
Close to the Earth	57
The Patriot	63
The Coloured Bangles	73

The Return

In single file the yoked bullocks amble down the parallel strips of cart road. An occasional car whizzes past, the whirl of dust whipped up by speeding tyres mingling with the lazy haze hanging over the leisurely convoy. The carts are empty, except the first, which carries a woman wedged into the inverted apex of matting over crossed bamboo. Somewhere down the line of carts a man is singing softly. The dust and the melody are rich with the flavour of a forgotten past. The young cart driver is still trying to maintain the one-sided conversation.

"I used to own some land close to the lake. It's good land."

The woman says nothing.

It came to me as part of my wife's dowry. But I exchanged it with land or the other side of the railway crossing, nearer my own."

"There is no need to be nervous, she is thinking. No one will recognise me.

"Have you ever seen a sugar factory?" he asks after a while.

"Yes."

Raju had taken her once, in spite of the disapproval of the whole village. Raju had been like that. The opinion of others had never affected him. She had watched the load of sugar cane being fed into the voracious innards of the gigantic machine. The ground beneath her feet had trembled with the rumble and clank of the metal monster. Raju had ben furious when she had flirted with the man in charge and flattered and wheedled him into taking her right to the top. He didn't speak to her all the way home. But the next day he had forgotten his temper. Raju could never remain angry for long.

"It's an impressive sight, isn't it?" the young cart driver is asking.

"Yes."

"We have just been to the sugar mill. We go regularly. To sell our cane, you know. I had a good load this time. Almost ten quintals."

The woman is lost in memories.

"I don't only grow cane, you know," the young cart driver's voice intrudes on her thoughts.

"Oh." The word is flat, discouraging talk. But he is greatly encouraged by the monosyllabic response.

"That's right. Last month I sold Rs. 150 worth of mustard."

The dust and the melody. Suniya the Shameless, branded from birth, willful enough to justify the branding. No, there can be no return. Just a sorry compromise.

"My wife is allergic to mustard," the young cart driver is saying. "Isn't it funny that I should surround myself with what she's allergic to?" He laughs at his sally.

So much greenery on either side. Green fields against the brown earth. Like the emerald glowing against the palm of Lal Chand's sister. "It was a bad colour for an emerald," Sher Singh had said when she raged against the gift. "It was pointless selling it, and how could I have given you such an inferior quality stone?" That was the day she had known, and they had all known, that her days as Sher Singh's woman were numbered.

"Actually, she is constantly nagging me to grow something else on that land." The young cart driver is still intent on his mustard. "But I tell her not to be silly. She will get used to my mustard. I get a good price for it. Besides, I have always grown mustard on that land. We're near the lake now. You can't see it from the road, but it's there to your left. Beyond that clump of sugar cane."

Her eyes strain towards the left. Everything looks so different. She would not have found the place on her own.

The cart driver is looking at her curiously.

"Your family lives here?"

Family. One blind man, one boy grown to manhood.

"I have no family."

"It's a long distance to travel to visit nobody."

Her colourful bundle is clutched under her arm. She clambers down with difficulty. For a brief moment she stands uncertainly by the side of the road.

"Well, old woman, God grant you peace."

The Return

Now that she will no longer have to hear his chatter, she can smile at him. The smile brings a flash of beauty to her ravaged face.

"Thank you, my son. God be with you."

The convoy moves on, the belled bullocks clanking hollowly, each man in turn gazing with idle curiousity at the drab figure walking slowly towards the setting sun. Suniya the Shameless returning to her village with predictable humility.

Through the field of yellow-green mustard, past the tall sugar cane, down to the very edge of the slime-edged, mirrored stillness. And there in the middle of the lake, the same frail craft. No, surely not the same, but so like it. She and Raju in the hot afternoon sunlight, insecurely afloat on an uncertain craft. "Never mind them, Suniya. Maybe your mother was a whore. I do not know of such things. But you are a good girl. I know it." But that, too, was before the accident. Afterwards his sightless eyes had disgusted her. Besides, there were so many goodlooking boys in the village, and she had always known that she was very beautiful.

She walks slowly round the side of the lake. At least she has the compromise. She stops to watch children chase a stray cow home. A handful of adults dribble homewards from the fields. Suniya has reached the little temple. This is where she plans to build her hut. Close to the village, but not part of it. Her compromise. She can never again be a part of that village.

She can see the village from where she sits. Thatch atop baked mud huts, huddled together, growing like a wart from the cleft in the lake. She opens her gaily patterned bundle and takes out the last of her chapattis. If only he had not been so gentle, so patient, so blind.

"I will not marry him. He is blind."

"You have no choice, you slut. No other man in the whole village is willing to have you."

"No other girl in the whole village is willing to have him!" she had replied with spirit. "While I can name dozens whose tongues hang out at sight of me."

"Aye dozens! Those dozens only pant to take you out among the tall cane. Maybe they already have. But marriage! I could tie a queen's dowry round your neck and no one would have you."

Blind Raju, her one-time friend, a gentle, hopelessly considerate husband.

"I am very beautiful, you know," she had said to him.

"I know."

"How do you know!" she taunted him contemptuously. "You are blind."

The nerve at the corner of his mouth had twitched. She was to see that nerve throb many times.

"I have known you a long time, remember?" he had replied gently. "You were always beautiful."

"But never as beautiful as I am now. Dhanno says that the moon is ashamed to show its face in front of me."

His face had darkened but his voice had remained even.

"Suniya, you should not let other men comment on your beauty."

"Then who will? You? You can't even see it."

He must have known, there were plenty of people to tell him, how she would swagger down to the village well, flaunting her beauty with a toss of her unveiled head, with a swing to her insolent hips, with a deliberately wanton sway to deliberately provocative walk. Not even motherhood had been able to blunt her animal magnetism.

The chill evening air sweeps up from the lake. She shivers. Inside the village the many fires must be warm and comforting. It is dark enough for her to begin her pilgrimage. A foolish woman in search of fragments of a long shattered past.

She walks towards the village. Round the blank impassive mud walls, down pathways beaten smooth by the feet of unchanged decades. A child is crying piteously. Its mother picks it up, smacks its bare bottom and bundles it into a dimly lit interior. Further down, a hut with a single brick wall. Old Jaggan's hut. He has obviously prospered. Not old Jaggan. He must be dead. His fat-fingered son.

She stops by a broken stone pillar and looks for her old drawing of a bullock cart. It is still there, barely visible in the dusky half light. She rubs it with a corner of her veil. She cannot erase it. Let this bit of her past remain forever. Suniya the Shameless has faded with her youth. Left is a world-soiled pilgrim staring at an indelible drawing.

There is no one at the well. She runs her hand down the smooth surface of the pulley post where Sher Singh lounged so indolently. Virile. That was the word for Sher Singh. Big, burly and massive shouldered, with undisguised lust in his heavy browed eyes. So different to the surreptitious wetting of lips of the village menfolk.

The Return

Sher Singh, the feared, the Daku, who had materialised from nowhere. A ferocious Punjabi so far from his native soil. And she had been the only one in the village unafraid of him. She had only meant to add him to her list of conquests. She hadn't bargained for her tempestuous response to his aggressive masculinity. Then one night she had left her patient Raju, had left her beloved Munna, and, mindless in the depth of her passion, had run away with Sher Singh. Now, standing by the well, she can see the nerve throb at the corner of blind Raju's mouth. And throb. And throb. She presses her hand against her eyes.

She slides her hand over the rough taut rope and raises the wooden bucket from the well. How sweet the water. Better than her first silver bangles, better than the homage of the Daku band, better than an emerald glowing on a brown palm. It had taken her all the remaining years of her youth to realise that there is no place in a big city for the one-time woman of a celebrated Daku. Too late. There can be no return. Not ever. She's lucky to have the compromise.

The beaten path is solid and comforting beneath her feet. A woman passes by and stares curiously. But Suniya is veiled. In any case no one will know her.

In front of the hut sits an old man. Blind eyes set in a patient unchanged face. She never loved him, so why does she cry? He knows someone stands before him because he has pushed away his hookah. Let him not ask who she is. If she speaks even to lie he will recognise her voice. He must not force her to go. Not yet. Not till she has seen her Munna. Her Munna who was a boy and is now a man. Married, perhaps, with sons of his own. She knows now that she can never live by that temple. Not so close to lost happiness. The compromise was a delusion. One last time she will look at her Munna, then she will go away. Forever.

She steps past him trying to peer into the hut. With that step he is sure of the footsteps he thought he recognised. And then she hears his voice, warm with joy, call "Bahu! Your mother-in-law is here and awaits your obeisance."

Uma

The Vedic chants were soothing, melodious. The crackle of the sacred fire dispelled the chill of the evening. Under the heavy veils her ugly face was radiant.

Uma the unwanted was, miraculously, Uma the bride.

Seven times round the fire. Small, slow steps, the trailing sari, the halting progress, disguising her limp.

Enshrouded by her illusions, Uma was unaware of the deceit she perpetrated.

The wailing shehnais saw the bemused bride off. There were no real tears. Only the flood of hypocrisy dictated by tradition.

Uma's mother alone wept in sorrow. Such a good match wasted on the undeserving Uma.

The raucous band hired by the Barat ushered the bride into her new home. The widowed mother gazed with pride at her handsome son Ranjit and sighed with satisfaction at the thought of the lovely bride concealed beneath the heavy veils. She had dreamed of this day for many years. Such a beauty, she thought to herself, was worth relinquishing the handsome dowries she had been offered.

Oil was poured in the doorway before the bride; all the auspicious rituals were taken care of. The widow guided her new daughter-in-law into the brightly lit interior. It was late. The relatives and guests were tired. The bride was shown into the flower-bedecked bridal chamber.

She was still veiled. The illusion persisted.

Ranjit, the groom, lingered over the last farewells. The guests departed, the red glow of his cigarette was the only answer to the gay sparkle interlacing the festive trees. He flicked his half-smoked cigarette out into the cool darkness of the night and went in to his bride.

She sat on the bed, a shapeless tent of shimmering red silk, framed by the delicate chameli flowers. Involuntarily his hand touched his achkan pocket and the memory of the familiar photograph rose before his eyes. The fragile, childish features he had grown to love were separated from his touch only by a length of red silk.

He crossed over to her and gently, tenderly, lifted the veil which obscured the downcast face.

And then the horror hit him.

The pock-marked face was a mockery against the soft fabric that framed it, and the comparison with the picture in his pocket tasted bitter. Anger mounted as he realised the shameful trick played on him and his mother.

Suppressing his blinding fury, he commanded, "Look at me."

Uma looked up slowly, her eyes dwelling on the length of him, on the smoldering fire in his eyes. She drank in each detail of this man who had chosen her, who alone had ever wanted her. Her hopes and her longings had stripped her of all her defences and all the vulnerability of the sensitive woman was in her eyes. She revealed to him eyes aged by humiliation, by rejection, by pain; eyes made luminous by her unshakable faith in the goodness of this man, her husband, who stood before her.

Her eyes shook him. He could not hurt her. His anger died, stillborn. He looked at her eyes and he asked gently, "What is your name?"

"Uma," she replied.

His gaze shifted to the rest of her face. Unable to bring himself to touch her, he sat next to her on the bed. His mind was dulled with shock.

And as she waited, she grew more afraid. Is it possible that he didn't know, she thought to herself, or am I even worse than the description they gave of me.

She waited for him to say something, anything. Then at last the words were wrung out of her.

"Did they tell you, did you know, that I was ugly?"

He saw the whipped look in her eyes, and he was overwhelmed with pity. At last he took her hand and there was a promise of friendship in the warmth of his touch.

"It doesn't matter," he said simply. "You are my wife and I have accepted you."

With this she was content.

Long after she fell asleep Ranjit lay awake. Towards the early hours of the morning he switched on the lamp and drew out the cherished photograph. He looked at it a long time. Then he lit a match and watched the photograph burn to a heap of ashes.

The next morning while Uma bathed and dressed he went to his mother.

"Ammaji," he said, "Ram Bhatnagar switched brides. He has sent us his eldest daughter instead of the one we chose."

Ammaji's eyes were wide with disbelief.

"The ugly one?" she whispered.

"Yes," he replied.

She sat down suddenly, bereft of speech.

"I'm convinced she knows nothing about her father's duplicity," continued Ranjit, "and you must not tell her."

"Must not tell her!" echoed his mother, her eyes flashing militantly. "You think she knows nothing of it? You think they could have done this shameful thing without her knowledge and consent? Oh my poor innocent boy! Why the whole world knows how hard they tried to find a suitor for her. They would have married her to a sweeper had they got him to agree to take her off their hands! I warned you. I told you the family was a worthless bunyah family, but no. You had to set your heart on a pretty face glimpsed at a crowded wedding. 'Find our who she is, Ammaji'," she mimicked, 'I will marry only her'. Stubborn and headstrong. That's what you always were! I don't know who you inherit it from. Your father, poor man, was so gentle and reasonable! Well, there's your Sunita! There's the girl you chose. Such wonderful proposals, such sizable dowries, all flung to the winds!"

"That's enough!" snapped Ranjit. "I didn't come to listen to your interminable lectures."

She was afraid of her son. Instantly meek, she said in a conciliatory tone, "You are right. What is done is done. It's not such a calamity. I can still line up a dozen beautiful brides from good families for you to choose from. Have you sent her back?"

It was his turn to stare at her in disbelief.

"Ammaji!" he said, shocked. "She's my wife. Send her where?"

"She's not your wife. A marriage by deceit is no marriage at all. Send her back to her parents immediately. Where is that she-demon? I will pull her by her hair and throw her out."

"Ammaji!" He was really angry now. "I never thought I'd ever hear you speak like this. She, poor thing, is herself the innocent victim of a cruel fate. More important, she is my wife. I married her before a thousand witnesses and before God. What are you saying?"

"Listen, Ranjit," said Ammaji patiently, "we are not expected to keep her. Not even by her parents. They know we will send her back, but now that she's married, it doesn't matter. They have got rid of the stigma of a spinster daughter in the family. The path has been cleared for the marriage of the younger girls. They expect us to send her back. Really, I should have suspected something when they accepted with such alacrity the proposal we sent for Sunita. But I was so immersed in your desires, and, quite frankly, I thought that an offer from a family like ours was enough to make them override all thoughts of custom and tradition. Well they have removed the stigma from their family by throwing it on our shoulders, we must remove the stigma from ours. To avoid the derision of the world we must send her back immediately. I'll arrange the second wedding within a fortnight. I will choose a bride from amongst the finest families. A daughter-in-law is a symbol of a family's good fortune and prestige. I can't keep that . . . that cripple in the family! She will bring nothing but disaster. I know it! She was born under an unlucky star. It would be foolish to keep her.

Ranjit waited patiently till she finished.

"I'm sorry you feel like this Ammaji," he said firmly. "She is my wife before God and nothing can change that. I have accepted her, and I want you to do the same. I will bring her to you in a little while. See that you treat her well."

Though seething with righteous anger, Ammaji was too afraid to defy her son. It was easy for him to accept her, she thought bitterly. He need never see her except in the dark. But I'll have her inauspicious face before me every minute of the day. My friends will laugh at me, delight in my bad fortune. To think that since he was born I used to dream of the daughter-in-law I would bring home one day! Oh that dream of a slim girl weaving gracefully through the house with a bunch of keys dangling from her young hips, with her dainty feet moving to the tinkle of her anklet bells!

She was prepared, but when she saw the ugliness of her club-footed daughter-in-law, her palms itched to slap the deceitful face. But Uma's eyes were moist with gratitude. This was the woman who had chosen her above her beautiful sisters. All the devotion of her generous nature was in her heart, in her fingertips, as she bent to touch the feet of her mother-in-law. Conscious of her son's stern eyes, Ammaji publicly acknowledged her daughter-in-law's obeisance with a show of grace. She heard the sniggers with hardening bitterness. She would have her revenge. She couldn't throw out this hideous girl, but she would make her leave of her own accord.

She lost no time. Subtly at first, the poisoned darts picked their venomous way into the unwanted girl's consciousness. To begin with, Uma ignored the barbs. She told herself that they were a natural reaction to the sight of her deformed body. She merely doubled her efforts to please.

Besides, she had every reason to be content. She was with child. Her joy was stamped on the serenity of her narrow forehead. It infuriated Ammaji, whose hate became unbridled.

Her poisonous tongue grew more potent, the barbs more pointed. The hurt penetrated deeper each day, and Uma's devotion began to wilt under the frequency of the attacks. Shadows of unhappiness began to form around her and she desperately hugged to herself her one illusion. She was Uma the Chosen. Nothing could change that.

Till one day the last of her illusions crumbled before her.

It was summer. Big with child, Uma sat uncomfortably perched on the low wicker stool. After an hour of hard work the mountain of unripe mangoes looked discouragingly undiminished. She put down her knife and wiped her perspiring forehead with a corner of her sari.

"Daydreaming again!" snapped Ammaji, making one of her sudden disconcerting appearances. "One would think that being aware of your own obvious shortcomings you would at least make up for them by hard work. But no. Whenever one sees you, you are sitting with that foolish expression on your face. The lord only knows what terrible sins I committed to deserve such an affliction!"

Uma flushed with shame as she picked up her knife. She was too honest not to acknowledge the truth of that remark. She reminded herself once again that but for the goodness of this tight-lipped woman, she would still be in her parent's home, unwanted and reviled, a stumbling block to the marriage and happiness of her sisters.

Ammaji picked up another knife and joined Uma in paring the

eternal mangoes. And all the while she continued her vindictive mumbling.

" . . . and all the greatest beauties in the biradari had been offered to my son—together with such enticing dowries! And now I have this deformed creature on my hands to look at who is inauspicious. Cover your hideous face, girl, or you might sour the mango chutney."

Uma obediently veiled her face with her sari while an unfamiliar slow rage made her hands quiver.

"And the child she's carrying!" continued Ammaji with calculated malice. "I wonder what kind of a hideous monster it will be."

The impotent tears gushed to the surface. Goaded beyond endurance, Uma burst out.

"But nobody forced me on you or on your son. Why did you choose me? Why? So I could bear your son monster children?"

Ammaji put down her knife. Triumphant satisfaction lighted her face. Oh God, thought Uma in sudden fear, why did I ask that question. This is the question she has been goading me towards these last many months.

"Ranjit told me not to tell you," said Ammaji, "but now that you have asked me . . . " she shrugged her ample shoulders. Her eyes narrowed with hate.

"How could you imagine for one minute that I could ever choose you for my handsome son! It was your sister that they showed me. Yes. Now you know. They showed me your beautiful sister and married you off instead. We were tricked, you hear! We were tricked by your cheating, lying parents." She jabbed the mango viciously. "Next morning when Ranjit told me of the shameful trick, I wanted to send you back. Nobody would have questioned the justice of my decision. I could still have lined up a thousand pretty girls for my son. But no. He wouldn't have it. I can't understand him! So handsome, England returned, master of a prosperous ice factory, such a good catch, tied to a hideous piece of deformity. Don't give me that look of injured innocence. As if you didn't know! You knew what your parents were doing. You know what they have done to my son. You are responsible! You are twisted within and twisted without. You are a cunning, scheming monster and you have worked your viperous magic round my son and he can never be rid of you!"

Stunning waves of shock. The last of Uma's defences crumbled. She, the chosen one, crouched on the little stool while her illusions fell about her.

Her husband had been cruelly tricked. He had expected a beauty and had been confronted by her. And such was the goodness of her man that he kept his bitter disappointment to himself. He could have turned her out that very night but instead he had handled her gently and accepted her in all her ugliness.

In the wake of her fallen illusions came overwhelming gratitude. Not even the devotion of a life time could repay this debt. The little pride that she had acquired in the past months slipped away from her as she shouldered the knowledge of the debt she could never repay and redoubled her efforts to please, to serve, to anticipate every whim of this man who had accepted her.

A month later her child was born; perfect, without a blemish or even a wrinkle, with the glow of health on his delicate skin. She cradled the precious life in her arms and wondered at his beauty, which had been created from within her own twisted body. The little head nestled close, the hungry mouth sucked avidly. This was child. He would accept her love in all its unwanted abundance. Her child, the only being who needed her and would love her in return. In his world there would be no ugliness, no deformity. At last her life acquired the meaning it had never had. In her child she was complete.

Then followed the happiest days she was ever to know. Her child, the precious grandson, earned her a grudging respect. The barbs were withdrawn and she, the mother of her child, was sacred for a while.

Her child grew, thriving on the love and attention heaped on him. Uma loved, and was loved in turn. The little face lit up at the sight of her, little arms stole round her neck, and the call of her child wove a haven of sweetness for her bruised spirit. She spent more and more time with him, guarded him jealously, possessively, and saw little of the rest of the household.

Ranjit observed and was unhappy. Her voluntary exile from human contact was eloquent of the rejection and humiliation she had suffered. He had grown fond of her and liked her gentle, unobtrusive ways, knew her great virtues and wanted her to find acceptance in the eyes of her tormentors. He became obsessed with the idea of her gaining acceptance and recognition, and at last came up with a solution.

"Uma," he said to her one day, "every time I see you, you are sitting alone. Why do you shy away from the company of others? Why do you cringe every time they speak to you? Why do you humiliate yourself so? Is it because of your deformity? No, don't wince. You are deformed. You know it, and I know it. But whereas I accept it, you cannot do so. And you will never accept it because you only see yourself with the eyes of the world. It worries me, and I have at last found a solution. If, to prove your worth to yourself, you have to prove your worth to the world, then that is exactly what we must set out to do. I think that the best field for you is social work. You must gain recognition there, and only after people recognise you will you recognise yourself, and gain the confidence your lack."

Uma was startled and perturbed and marshalled up a battery of protests, but Ranjit could not be swayed. He had decided.

"I know that the idea of throwing yourself into the public eye scares you," he said. "But you must do it, Uma. I wish it."

"But I don't know the first thing about social work," she protested desperately.

"There's nothing difficult about social work. I have been making inquiries. There is a slum close by. It's a good place to start. Go and see how they live and you will know how you can help them."

"But I couldn't! I'm happy as I am. Really I am. I wasn't aware that I cringe. I'll mix more. Really I will."

"Uma," he said gently, "this is not some sort of a punishment I have devised for you. I'm only trying to help you. I know what I am doing. It is not normal to only want the company of a little baby. You are very lonely. I want to give you a little self-confidence. You are my wife and a great lady. It hurts me to see them snigger at you. I want your name to become a household word. People will come and touch your feet where before they ridiculed you. You will see how right I was in pushing you into this."

She could have fought harder against his decision, but she could not fight her gratitude. So she bowed her head in submission. She would do as he wished. It was a way to repay the debt.

The next morning she went to the slum. Painfully shy, she was acutely conscious of the eyes drinking in her deformity, lingering on her pitted skin, marking the clumsy uneven rhythm of her walk. The naked children clustered round, silent, curious, their sweating bodies caked with dust.

She didn't know where to begin, how to begin. Helplessly she approached the nearest woman.

"I've come to see if I can help you in any way," she fumbled for the right words and her eyes pleaded for understanding.

The woman stared at her. Drawn by curiosity, the other women drew closer.

"I would like to help you if I can," Uma began again. "Is there anything you need, anything I can do for you?"

And then they all began to talk together. The poverty and the need of these women assailed her from every side till she forgot her awkward body and listened only to the sorrow of their lives.

"Behanji," they said, "what is it that we do not need! We have no water. We walk many miles to collect our meagre supply. The government has promised to install a hand pump if we can raise half the money required. But we can barely feed our children. Where will we find the money for the pump?"

"Behanji!" said another, a young woman, "we have no latrines. We have to go out into the wilderness and we always go in groups of threes and fours because a lone woman is always molested."

"Behanji! If there were only a school we could send our children to! If we could only educate them and knew that life would offer more to them than we ever had."

Uma listened to the many women, and at night she brought their problems to her husband.

"We will handle the question of the pump first," he said immediately. "I will give you a list of all the leading families in Delhi. Tommorow you will call on them and collect funds for the pump."

Uma's public life had begun. She fought her agonising self-consciousness and willed herself into the offices of strangers, faced the many women, hostile against demands of charity, and she collected the money required. The hand pump was installed. A little later the simple arrangements for the latrines were made, a government grant was procured for a primary school close by and CARE was weedled into providing a free supply of milk on a daily ration basis. She spent most of the day in the dust of the slums. She taught the women simple acts of sanitation, she wiped their children's noses clean, and all the while she thought of her son, of the joy she was denying herself, of the attention she was depriving him of.

And each day her son grew to need her less. Deprived of his mother, he turned to his ever present grandmother who was overjoyed at this unexpected opportunity to sharpen her hate.

Slowly Uma's reputation spread and the demands on her time increased. Her days were spent in the slums and the villages, and her mornings and evenings were taken up by the many suppliants who waited with joined palms on the front veranda.

"Behanji, they have dispossessed me of my stall."

"Behanji, I am without a job, help me!"

"Behanji, I have been wronged."

The more her reputation grew, the harder her husband drove her. Her gratitude and the knowledge of her debt spurred her on. In her meagre free hours she tried to woo her son, but her wooing was infrequent and he was disinterested in the stranger she had become. She watched her son grow into a hardy school boy, and she had no time to share the secret joys and sorrows of his new world. She sensed his aloofness, but was confident that she would be able to win back his affection. Let her pay back her debt, let her ease the load of gratitude. There would still be time to heal the neglect of the past. Nature binds the mother and child with ties too strong to break. Let this madness pass, let her husband be content, and she would be able to return home to her child. She waited patiently for her husband's whim to find satiation.

But somewhere along the years the whim had changed to ambition and there could be no satiation. The name she had earned for herself by her social work was no longer the goal. It was merely a stepping stone to greater heights.

Her schoolboy son grew to adolescence, and as he grew, his impressionable mind bore the fruit of his grandmother's hate. "Such a mother is worse than no mother at all. You could die and she would never know. She is so busy with her outside affairs," and "poor little motherless boy! Your mother doesn't care for you. But I care. Come let me bandage your hurt and give you a sweetmeat."

Uma sat in her many villages while each day her son learnt to hate her more. She waited to repay her debt, positive that when she went to find him he would hear the call of her blood. The debt was almost repaid; her happiness could wait. Her son would understand.

Uma

Uma was now a name of great repute. The time was approaching for the realization of Ranjit's ambitions. The elections were drawing closer. By contacts, by bribery, Ranjit had procured a ticket. Then and only then did he divulge to Uma the extent of his ambitions.

"Uma," he said one night. "I think the time is ripe. You should contest these elections."

"Elections! whatever for? I have no interest in politics. I only want to be a housewife and a mother. I was going to speak to you too. I think I have done enough social work. The goal was reached long ago. Now I only want to be left in peace."

"No, my foolish Uma. The goal is only now in sight. I shall seat you among the stars. You have done very well for yourself. Yo must not think of quitting now. You are so well known in this constituency that these elections will be a walk-over for you."

"I am not interested," she said firmly. The debt was paid, gratitude was diminishing. The time had come to assert her own desires. "I think I have done enough. For these last nineteen yeas I have sacrificed my home at the altar of a public image. The image has been created—solid and unshakable. I have fulfilled your desires. Now I want to fulfill my own."

"You don't even know what you desire," he said irritably. "Your true sphere is your work. You have proved it. Why do you want to waste the labour of nineteen years? Now is the time to harvest the crop. Besides, I have already secured a party ticket for you. You must stand."

Nineteen years of submission. The habit was too hard to break. If he cared for her, she thought bitterly, he would have released her from this awful burden long ago. It was not her he thought of. It was his own ambition. All these years of gratitude, all her hopes and aspirations burnt at the feet of this man who had used her overwhelming gratitude against her.

But there was still her son. Embittered and poisoned though he was, he was still her son. No poison can work against a mother's love. She would seek out her son tomorrow. She was through with this life of public imagery. She had come home to her son.

She cornered her son while he ate a quick breakfast before going to college.

"Rajiv," she said, "your father wants me to stand for the Lok Sabha."

Her son looked at her impersonally.

"That must suit your own wishes admirably."

"Rajiv, it is not I who want to stand."

"Just as it has never been you who has wanted to create that public image," he responded bitterly. "I suppose you are going to say that you were an unwilling tool in Father's hands. You can't fool me! My father is gentle and good and unresisting. You have made a mockery of his love, you have made a mockery of your motherhood. You have never cared for any one or anything but your own image. Now you come to dupe me, to turn me against my father—the only parent I have ever known. What kind of a woman are you! Be satisfied that you have what you want and at least leave me my father!"

She sat stunned and disbelieving. He hadn't even given her a chance. Her mother's heart had found no echo in him.

"Rajiv!" She held out her hand like the blind. The pain was in her voice, in her deeply expressive eyes, in the yearning of her fingers. "I have loved you like no woman could love her child. I have wept for all the years I have had to hold myself aloof. I gazed at your sleeping face night after night and have despaired over my lost joy. You are my only reason for existence. But first I had to repay my debt. Believe me, it was your father who wished it. I wanted nothing. Only you."

"Grandmother was right." His voice was choked with anger. "What honey drips from your tongue! But you will never fool me. I am on my guard against you. You have shattered my father, but you will never break me. Go to your villages. Go to where you sowed your love. There is nothing here that you can claim. You have no son. You only have an army of villagers!"

The door banged with the finality of his departure. She heard the angry roar of his motor cycle. A fly buzzed about her head. The happiness she had promised herself lay shattered around her. Her son was lost to her. He, too, had rejected her. There was nothing left for her here. Gratitude was gone, the debt had been paid in full. Uma the unwanted sat alone.

The Wolf At The Door

They met at a party.

She was easily the most attractive girl there. Brimming with bubbling vivacity, she was the centre of a group of laughing youngsters. He naturally gravitated towards her.

"That beautiful music is being wasted," he murmured behind her. "Would you care to dance?"

She turned to look at him. He looked deliciously self-possessed and sophisticated.

"I'd love to," she replied.

He was a good dancer. She surrendered to the rhythm of the music and to the firm, sure steps of her partner. They didn't talk at all.

"May I get you a drink?" he asked when the music ended.

"Thank you, no," she smiled. "There is a limit to the number of cokes I can consume in one evening."

"Try something else for a change. No? Well, wait here while I get myself a drink. Don't disappear. I want to talk to you. It took a lot of planning to extricate you from that crowd."

He was back in a minute and sat down beside her. It was pleasantly cool on the lawn.

"I still haven't introduced myself," he said. "I'm Vivek Anand."

"I'm Meera Ahuja."

"I've always liked the name Meera. There is a lilt to it and it suits you. I like your name, I like your face, and I like the way you dance. It's a good beginning."

Careful Meera, she told herself. This is an animal outside of your experience. This is a Wolf.

"Steady on the compliments," she cautioned. "You're rocking the boat and I'm out of my depth."

"And that's exactly where I want you to be," he declared. "Will you have dinner with me tomorrow night?"

"I don't know," she said doubtfully.

"Now that's a very silly answer. Very unworthy of you. Either you want to, or you don't."

"Even if I wanted to, I couldn't say yes straight away. I must ask my parents."

"Ask your parents!" he exclaimed, astounded. "How old are you?"

"Twenty-two."

"And you still have to ask your parents?"

She flushed, but held her ground.

"I don't suppose they'd refuse. It's just that the question has never arisen. I often go out to dinner parties, but I have never wanted to go out alone with a man before."

"And now?" he asked softly.

"As I said, I don't know. I think I'm a little afraid of you," she confessed.

He looked exaggeratedly flattered.

"That's the most encouraging thing you've said to me all evening. In fact, that settles the question. I'll pick you up at eight."

He was laughing at her and she knew it. He was undeniably attractive. It would be fun to go out with him, she thought suddenly.

"Thank you," she said, "I'll be ready." She hesitated a moment before adding, "Would it be possible for you to come half an hour earlier? I'm sure my parents would like to meet you."

"Oh oh," he said, "I didn't realize I'd need to be screened so carefully."

"Naturally," she said tartly. "Would you let your daughter go out with a complete stranger? One who might well turn out to be a dastardly Wolf?"

"I don't have a daughter," he reminded her mildly.

"Well, you will one day," she concluded, as she gathered up her purse and smiled a sweet farewell.

As he watched her leave, he thought with sudden dismay, she's really too young for me. Too young, too sweet, too innocent. Not the type to enter into the spirit of the game. What have I let myself in for!

Even so, he dressed with greater care the following evening. Looking at himself critically in the mirror, he was sorry he didn't wear glasses. There was something reassuring about a man who wore glasses. He frowned at his image. Now, would I let my daughter go out with a man who looked like that? Dammit, that little school miss is brain-washing me!

He arrived at her house punctually at seven thirty, but waited another five minutes in the car. It was bad strategy to arrive exactly on time, he told himself. He was given a cordial welcome by her parents, and was handed a drink before he was subjected to a politely worded but very thorough interrogation. There's not much more they can ask me, he reflected finally. They know almost as much about me as I know about myself. It was with relief that he saw Meera rise, ready to leave at last. He had passed the test.

She looked smug and contented as she settled herself in the car beside him. His look of amused sarcasm was lost on her.

But the evening more than made up for the earlier cross-examination. She was quick witted, intelligent, and intensely alive, and it was a pleasure to watch her mobile face register each fleeting impression. It was with regret that he dropped her home that evening.

"I have two tickets for the cricket match tomorrow," he said as he helped her secure the gate. "Will you come?"

"Oh yes, I'd love to," she said, her face lighting up with glad acceptance.

"Good, I'll pick you up at eleven."

She hadn't the faintest idea of the game, and was terribly distracting to be with.

"Let's confuse them by tossing in a couple of extra balls," she whispered.

He frowned at her.

"Well, it's such an exasperatingly slow game," she said defensively.

He bought her a bag of pop corn. It kept her occupied for a while.

"Me, I like tennis," she announced, crumpling up the empty polythene bag. "It's fun to watch all the heads turn from side to side in unison."

"It's such a joy to discover what a sport's fan you are," he said acidly. "Come on. I'll take you to a more stimulating place. That is," he added as an afterthought, "if you don't want to wait to get the cricketers' autographs."

"Oh!" She clapped her hand to her mouth in mock horror, "That's what I forgot to bring! My autograph book!"

He grinned at her. They went to a Jerry Lewis film.

It wasn't till much later that he asked her a question that had been puzzling him.

"Tell me, how is it that you've reached the ripe old age of twenty-two without ever wanting to go out for dinner with any man."

"There's nothing very mysterious about that," she laughed. "It's just that every man I've cared for hasn't cared for me, and vice versa. A continual history of unrequited love."

"And now?"

"And now I care for you and you care for me. It's as simple as that. Besides, it's added fun going out with you when I know that eventually I'm going to marry you."

He spluttered into his beer.

"Meera! Let's get this straightened out. I'm sorry if I gave you the wrong impression, but I'm just not the marrying kind."

"Stuff and nonsense," she said, unperturbed.

"Now wait a minute. No matter what you might feel to the contrary, no matter how hard you try to bulldoze me into anything, I'm not going to marry you. Not ever. And that's final."

"If you've finished trying to convince yourself," she said patiently, "would you please stop sprinkling beer on top of your hamburger. If you're looking for the bottle of tomato sauce, it's to your right."

Nothing could convince her that to him marriage was not an essential part of the fabric of life. Her reasoning was simple. Falling in love was a prelude to marriage. One was inevitably the outcome of the other. But to him, marriage was the complete annihilation of the individual, and he was first and foremost an extreme individualist. He understood what an alien he would be in her ordered, conventional world, and often warned himself that the time had come to put an end to their idyll. The longer he delayed, the sharper would be the hurt he dealt her. After all, she was twenty-two. Old enough to settle down. She'll make an excellent wife to a nice solid, steady man. Enliven up his life a bit, he chuckled.

But no matter how resolutely he planned the break, circumstances conspired to make him postpone the deed. First it was her approaching birthday, then she came down with 'flu. He gave her time to recover, then planned his strategy carefully. The evening he had selected was perfect for his purpose. They had half an hour alone before her parents returned from a cocktail party. Just enough time to permit the right amount of dramatics.

"Meera," he began, "I have been waiting for an opportunity to talk to you."

"Me too," she said, oblivious to the gravity in his voice, "and what you want to say couldn't be half as exciting as what I want to say." She paused dramatically. "I've written a story."

"Oh!" he said, taken aback.

"I have it here, hidden under the cushion, so I could show it to you immediately." She pulled it out, handed it to him with a triumphant flourish, and said, "If you can't decipher it, ask me."

And perched on the arm of his chair, looking alternately nonchalant and intensely involved, she waited impatiently for his verdict.

"Hm," he said, "not bad for a first attempt."

"What do you mean, not bad! It's terrific! Suppose I win the Nobel Prize one day—you'll feel pretty foolish having called it 'not bad' so condescendingly."

She was in such a fever of excitement over her story that he hadn't the heart to put his plan into action.

After that she abandoned herself into an orgy of writing, and her moods, always uncertain, now veered dizzily from one extreme to the other. She suffered from all the throes of depression and self-flaggellation budding authors subject themselves to, and he naturally couldn't abandon her in such an emotionally disturbed condition. The creative urge finally yielded to a positive mania for amateur dramatics. With incredible tenacity, she haunted every play-reading till at last her persistence was rewarded by an obscure part in a third-rate play. He sat with commendable patience through the incredibly bad play, which mercifully passed unnoticed by the press. Her dramatic talent thus unrecognised, she scornfully abandoned the ungrateful state, and, before her imagination could devise another soul-shaking career, he speedily launched the long planned break.

It was autumn. They were in an open car.

"How old are you?" he asked abruptly.

"Eighteen, going on to thirty-six," she answered rudely.

"Seriously, Meera. Let's see—it's a year since I first met you..."

"Stop beating around the bush. So I'm twenty-three. So what?"

"It's time you got married," he said.

"Hey!" she shouted joyfully, as she flung her arms around his neck. "That's what I've been saying all along. I thought you'd never ask me."

"Hold it! Hold it!" he said, extricating himself with difficulty. "I said it's time you got married. I didn't say to me. It's no use looking hurt. I'm a confirmed bachelor, and I like being that way. But that doesn't mean that I'm blind to your wifely potentialities. So that's why I'm going to give you a break. From now on, you are going husband hunting. Alone."

Her stricken face was a reproach more eloquent than words, and he hastened to put forward all his crushing arguments.

"I don't *want* to break with you, Meera. I love you. And because I love you, I want you to taste all the happiness life can give you. You are very young, still adaptable, still starry-eyed. Given a chance you'll easily find a worthier man. I'm thirty-two—almost ten years older than you. When you are forty-five, in the full possession of all your faculties, full of life, I'll be an old man—bedridden, woolly-headed, and a shameful drain on your energies. Even if you scoff at such a remote future, think of the present. I'm a selfish bachelor, too accustomed to my ways to change. I sit up half the night with a book, and the light is sure to disturb you. I'm a messy shaver, I splatter the bathroom deplorably when I bathe, I leave my clothes lying all over the place, my socks smell—you couldn't live with me! You're the nice orderly housewifely type, and I'd drive you round the bend. We'd destroy each other. Besides, I'm a terrible womanizer. Always have been, and can't change now," he concluded firmly.

She looked at him a long time. All the joy had left her.

"You really mean to leave me." It was a statement. The awful finality of it was dawning on her.

It occurred to him to protest against the word, to soft-talk the sting out of it, but the luminous courage of acceptance in her eyes shamed all subterfuge.

"Yes," he said.

Her voice was steady, without the faintest trace of a tremour, as she said, "Will you take me home, please?"

He turned the car and drove her home. There was pride and

dignity in her carriage as she opened the gate and walked up to the door. She didn't look back.

For many days he congratulated himself on the neat, clean break. He returned to his bachelor haunts and resumed his prowling, sniffing out attractive faces. But his eyes kept searching for the bubbling vivacity he had grown used to, and somehow all the attractive faces were pallid by comparison. He grew steadily more irritable and irrascible and bad tempered, till one day even his paragon cook-bearer resigned.

It was a shock to sober up the dead.

Understanding dawned at last. He was churlish because he was miserable, and he was miserable because somehow, somewhere, she had insinuated herself into his blood, and now he was incomplete without her. The truth could no longer be denied. With blinding clarity he realised that his bachelorhood had really ended the day he met her. Marriage had nothing to do with it . . .

So that day he went out and bought a ring. It was a small diamond ring made to fit a very slim finger.

He was glad that she had won.

Masterji

" . . . and you used to put two-anna bits into his briefcase," says the voice of my mother. "It was supposed to be a secret between you . . ."

But I am not listening. I don't need to listen. The years fall away and I remember. Clear, sharply etched, the picture rises before my eyes . . .

A little girl standing in the doorway, a beloved pillow clutched under her arm. The dining room is quiet except for the low murmur of Masterji's voice. Dust dances in a stray shaft of sunlight. Bhaiya is listening intently to Masterji's soft, almost inaudible voice. Didi's head is bent low over her copybook. The little girl inches forward. Bhaiya sees her and favours her with a droll downward pull of his lips, one eye closing owlishly in a huge, slow wink. But she has eyes only for Masterji. Any minute now he will become aware of her standing there, and she will be enveloped in that wonderful warm smile. She is breathless with anticipation. The room is quiet, except for the low murmur of his voice, the faint scratching of Didi's pencil.

He turns.

"Hullo little Radha!"

His eyes crinkle, the warm radiance of his smile engulfs her, his silken beard curves and falls.

She tries to make her eyes crinkle like his. It is terribly hard.

"Masterji," says Didi, "how do you spell 'bicycle'?"

His attention is captured again. But Radha is content. He has smiled at her, has said "hullo little Radha", has re-established the link between them. She wanders round the room, opening drawers, re-arranging the spoons, making an unsteady heap of the forks, and listens to the murmur of their voices—Bhaiya's Didi's and Masterji's—and never once does he tell her not to make so much noise.

Till Mummy comes.

"Radha!" Mummy's whisper is sibilant, startling against the clatter of the fork castle. "Didn't I tell you not to disturb Masterji? Come away at once."

The little girl's mouth opens to protest against the injustice of the accusation.

Masterji quickly says, "Let her remain, Behanji. She is not disturbing us. In fact, I was going to speak to you about her. She loves being around while we work, so won't you permit her to join us? She can sit here and draw or I could start her off on her ABC. She's almost four. She's not too young to learn."

Mummy looks doubtful. Her Radha is only a baby.

"Oh yes, Mummy, please!" begs the child.

Mummy shakes her head in amazement. "All right," she says, "I'll give you a book and pencil."

The golden afternoons come in happy succession. Her awkward fist learns to trace lines fraught with mystery. She writes with painstaking concentration, then triumphantly presents him with the fruits of her labour.

"Beautiful." The admiration in his voice is a heady intoxicant. "Simply beautiful. There is only one thing, little Radha. 'A' does not stand on his head with his feet up in the air. That is a very tiring position for him to be in. Make him again, this time with his feet on the ground—like this. Ah! Now he looks comfortable."

When did the little girl first hear that Masterji was very poor? He, certainly, never told her. He was always so gay, with he eyes twinkling and crinkling, his silken beard curving to the movement of his lips. He must have puzzled that first day he discovered the two-anna coin in his briefcase. Perhaps it was a daily puzzle and he spent his evenings wondering where they came from. Or perhaps he had known all along but pretended not to see till the day the little girl looked up with her hand still slipped inside the briefcase. She saw him watching her, saw the blurry mist in his eyes, saw that wonderful smile, felt the emotion welling out of him, and her eyes filled in response. But he never spoke of it and neither did she.

She did not know that the same day he took his collection of coins to her mother.

"Behanji," he said, "you have a daughter with a heart as large as the sky. Every day she slips something into my briefcase. She knows that I know, but doesn't speak of it, and neither do I. It is a great secret between us. I cannot possibly refuse her the joy of her daily gift. Nor do I want to. So I take it from her and would like to return it to you." And the big, gentle Sardar's eyes filled with tears as he emptied his fistful of coins on to the mother's astonished palm.

"So this is why she wanted all those two-anna bits," her mother murmured softly. Then she handed the coins back to the weeping master and her face was soft with pride as she said, "Take them. They are yours. I am proud of my daughter."

Of this conversation the little girl knew nothing. It was told to her when she found the faded photograph in the musty godown . . .

The white bearded Sardar taught the children for a year. Everytime he came there was the warm smile, the curve of the silken beard, the twinkle in the gay eyes. And each time the secret lay like a jewel in the impassive briefcase. All through that year he taught and he smiled and no one knew of the sorrow that was consuming his world. Of a wife, of a family, of a suffering too hard for him to bear.

One day after that year, the children were not called in to lessons. Nor the next day. Nor the next. The questions of their casual curiosity were easily stilled. Masterji had been called away on some urgent work. There was no telling when he would be back. The two older children were overjoyed and played all through the uninterrupted afternoons. Only the little girl would sometimes wander into the still dining room, touch the empty chair and watch the dust dance in the shaft of sunlight.

So many years, so many turbulent joys and sorrows. So much forgotten, so much to forget. Gone is little Radha, and gone forever is the majic that was Masterji.

I sit in the musty godown, fingering the faded photograph. My voice of minutes ago still rings in my ears:

"Mummy, who is this man?" And her reply, "That's Masterji. Goodness, I've even forgotten his name. You were too young to remember, but he used to teach you children when we were on Alipur Road. It's a sad story. He was a terribly harassed man in great financial straits, and, unfortunately, he was too proud to tell anyone of his troubles. I wish he had told me. I'm sure we could have helped him. One day he couldn't face the burden of his life anymore, so he jumped in front of an oncoming train and he died. Daddy and I went to his family as soon as we heard. We did what we could do to help them. I used to hear from his wife for many years after his death, then she ceased to write and I lost touch with them."

I look at the photograph. I see the way the silken beard curves and fall, I see the twinkling, crinkling eyes.

"You used to put two-anna bits into his briefcase," says my mother's voice. "It was supposed to be a secret between the two of you . . ."

But I am not listening. I don't need to listen. I remember. The years fall away, and I remember.

The Resurrection

Kamla hummed to herself as she trimmed the paan leaves with skilled precision. The shaded windows let in the hazy sounds of the autumn morning: the strong, even rhythm of the leaves being swept off the grass, the sharp chirrup of the sparrows mingled with the hoarse calls of the crows, the dull thud of the gardner's spade against the firm earth; murmured voices, the distant ringing of cycle-rickshaw bells, the buzz of the blue-bottle hovering in a shaft of sunlight. She loved this time of morning when, alone and undisturbed, she tended to her paan-daan. Her paan-daan reflected her love of perfection with its highly polished antique silver mirroring the betel-nut cut carefully into small, uniform pieces, the smooth creamy texture of the freshly prepared kattha, and the paan leaves wrapped up in the damp cloth waiting their turn to be trimmed with practised care. She was beautiful still, having aged gracefully, and her fair Kashmiri skin was unlined except for the fine lines etched round her eyes. She was absorbed and contented when the barefooted servant padded in to announce the arrival of her cousin Vimla.

"Vimla!" she exclaimed happily, as she rose to embrace her cousin. "What a lovely surprise! Why I haven't seen you for months! You look wonderfully well. Why haven't you been over to see me for so long, you wicked girl!"

If Vimla's answering smile was a little abstracted, it passed unnoticed. She settled herself comfortably on the divan opposite the gleaming paan-daan, and surveyed her cousin with affection.

"You know my brother-in-law was here with his family on a temporary posting, so I had a house full of guests. A lot of fun, but a lot of hard work, which is why I haven't been over for so long. You look well, Kamla didda. Well and happy and contented. I hear you are considering Jivan Bhai Tikku's son for Chand?"

"It's almost settled," replied Kamla contentedly. "Would you care for a paan? Ramu!" she called to the servant, "bring two glasses of cold sherbet and the fruit which I left on the pantry table."

Happy to have an opportunity to discuss the intricate details of the proposed wedding of her daughter, Kamla plunged into this absorbing topic.

"He is a fine boy, Jivan Bhai's son. For one so young, he has already built up quite a practice. The only thing I feel sorry about is that he has chosen to set up his practice in Lahore. I had deliberately chosen an Allahabad family so I could have my girls within reach. Anyway it is such a very desirable match that I must consent to sending my daughter to another city. I was planning to give Chand my pearl satlara as part of her trousseau. Apart from that, I plan to give her one gold set, one kundan set, and one other set of her choice. What do you think?"

"Good idea," said Vimla absently.

"And I plan to give her eleven sarees—or perhaps fifteen would be a better number. What do you think?"

"Humm?"

"Vimla, you haven't been listening! What's the matter? You seem very preoccupied."

"No, I'm listening," said Vimla with a guilty start.

"Something's on your mind. What is it, Vimla? Did you have a special reason for coming to see me?"

Vimla gazed at the tassel on the big bolster pillow with rapt attention.

"Well?" said Kamla.

Vimla still seemed to hesitate; then, her mind made up, she rushed into her story. "I went to a wedding yesterday. You know my friend, Sumitra?" she added with seeming irrelevance, "her sister's daughter's wedding."

She hesitated again.

"And . . . ", prompted Kamla, her curiosity aroused.

"Kamla didda, did you have another daughter? I mean apart from the three I know."

Something inside her seemed to squeeze her heart painfully. Will I never be able to master that old grief, thought Kamla to herself. How silly to weep at the mention of an old tragedy. She fought back the rush of tears and answered quietly.

"Yes, but she died many years ago. She was drowned in the Ganges at Hardwar when she was eight."

Vimla seemed to search for words.

"Kamla didda," she said finally, "suppose she is not dead."

"Vimla, please!" said Kamla greatly agitated. "If you have something to say, say it. Don't beat about the bush or play foolish games. It is too painful."

"She is not dead," said Vimla abruptly. "She's alive. I've met her."

There was a roaring in Kamla's ears. Her head felt light and very strange. The roaring passed and she could hear Vimla's voice again.

". . . and wants to meet you."

It was only then that Vimla noticed how pale and still Kamla had become.

"Kamla didda! Oh, I'm sorry. What a fool I am to throw a thunderbolt at you without preparing you for it. Ramu! Ramu! Pani lao!"

Kamla gestured unsteadily with her hand.

"It's alright. I'm alright. What did you say? My child—! Not dead? You've met her? Where? After so many years! Oh God! My little girl! I can't believe it!"

"It's true, Kamla didda. I've met her. At least I've met a girl who says she's your daughter. She says she was kidnapped by a sadhu in Hardwar when she was eight years old."

"Kidnapped! I thought she had drowned. We had gone together for a dip in the Ganges. I'd told her to stay close to me. I was praying, I never noticed. And I looked for her everywhere. I called and called. I made the men swim far out into the water, but there was no sign of her. I thought the swift current had carried her away. Oh God! After so many years! My child! Alive! Where is she? Where did you meet her? Why did you not bring her to me? Come. What are we waiting for? Take me to my child."

"Wait, Kamla didda. Sit down. You had better hear everything before you go."

"What is there to hear? My child who had died has come alive again. What greater joy can there be? Come, hurry up. Ramu! Have the landau brought to the gate."

"Kamla didda, wait! You must prepare yourself. Have you asked yourself where she must have been these last fifteen years?

What she has seen, what she had been?"

The joy in Kamla's face gave way to a glimmer of dreadful comprehension. "What do you mean?" she whispered. "What are you trying to say?"

"She is not like your other daughters, Kamla didda. She has not been sheltered, and protected, and reared in security. She has seen life at its harshest, life at its basest."

"Tell me!" It was a command.

"The sadhu who kidnapped her sold her into prostitution."

Kamla swayed with sick shock.

"It was not till many years later that she was able to run away," continued Vimla. "She begged for a while, then managed to join a group of singers. They wander from town to town. Having no money, not knowing where to look for you, many years and many towns having separated her from the past, she took to approaching every Kashmiri she met and asking them if they knew you. That's how I met her."

Kamla nodded. Her face showed her age.

"At Sumitra's sister's wedding?"

"At Sumitra's sister's wedding," Vimla affirmed. "There was this group of singers. They sang quite well. After the recital a young girl detached herself from the chorus and came across to me. 'Do you know Kamla—? she asked me. 'Yes,' I said, 'very well.' 'At last!' she said, as tears came to her eyes. 'Will you take me to her?' 'Why?' said I. 'Because she is my mother.' "

The tears came unashamedly. She was unaware of Vimla sitting there. She was unaware of the autumn sounds in the garden. She only saw a little girl with her hair pulled back into two tight plaits. A barefooted little girl playing with a big shaggy dog in the courtyard. A happy little girl with no conception of evil, sold to a life of horrible degradation. Her child. Her precious first-born, whose fragile girlhood had been cruelly crushed before it could flower.

"I must go to her." She stood up in desperate haste. "I must wipe out the horror of the past. I will bring her home . . . "

Bring her home. She stopped. A picture rose unbidden to her mind of her three daughters, simple, innocent, clothed in young dignity, and the shadowy figure of her fourth lost child emerged standing beside them. Her fourth, lost child draped in cheap tinsel—a prostitute! Goading her mind to accept the harsh reality of it, she repeated the word again. A prostitute!

The Resurrection

The Tikkus! What will be their reaction when they find out? Would I marry my son to a girl whose sister had been a prostitute? What will be the future of my other daughters. But how can I return this child so miraculously brought to life back to the misery she has endured these last fifteen years?

Her mind wracked with terrible conflict, she pushed open the wire netting and went out into the hot courtyard.

"Vimla!" she called. "Go home now. I want to be alone. I must think."

Vimla came out into the courtyard, embraced her cousin, and asked unhappily, "Was it wrong of me to have told you? Should I have kept quiet about the whole thing?"

"I don't know."

"Send for me if you need me."

Vimla went back through the wire netting door and let herself out of the house. Kamla continued to stand in the hot courtyard overlooking the shade-flecked orchard of malta trees.

During the day she watched her daughters, brought up to expect love, marriage, children, security, and comfortable happiness as their birthright. She listened to their unworldly chatter, their silly quarrels, and their unaffected laughter. It was their future, their birthright, weighed in the balance against the unhappy blighted life of her first-born. What should she choose? Had she the right to condemn her girls to social ostracism, to willfully watch them age to withered spinsterhood? It was unthinkable. But what about her poor crushed castoff first-born, who had suffered to terribly, and had sought her out with hope in her heart? What about her birthright! What about her arms that ached to hold her daughter, what of her heart that longed to claim her child with joyful recognition? She would fight the world to give her child back her happiness. Alone she could fight. But she was not alone.

In the evening she watched her husband as he drank his tea and wiped his moustache dry. She was on the verge of telling him of the terrible decision which had been thrust upon her. But the man she had lived with for twenty-five years suddenly seemed a stranger. Why, we scarcely know each other, she thought, startled. Apart from an intimate knowledge of each others' habits, what do we share? We have always remained in our separate worlds without sharing a single thought. He is my husband: an object. I am his wife: functional, with no separate identity. Now, in her hour of greatest need, she could not admit him to the stronghold of her emotions. This had to be her decision.

She watched him take his walking stick as he went out to stroll in the garden. She watched her youngest daughter run after him and slip her hand into his, turning up her bright face with some childish query. She heard the tuneful lilt in the voice of her second daughter as she called out to the maid-servant, and she watched her eldest daughter, Chand, efficiently spinning the handle of the sewing machine, intent on the fabric she was stitching. She watched her family, and she made her decision. It was the only decision open to her.

Next day she sent a message to Vimla. She was calm and very composed as she greeted Vimla and offered her a paan.

"You have reached a decision," said Vimla quietly.

Kamla nodded. Her face was sculptored marble.

"My daughter died fifteen years ago in Hardwar. I cannot bring her back to life."

Tea Leaves

The thin man in the dhoti had a surprisingly resonant voice. It was not the first time that he addressed this crowd. His fiery eloquence thundered above their heads and carried with perfect clarity to the grey-templed figure sitting relaxed and attentive, comfortably wedged behind the steering wheel of the company jeep.

It was a good tamasha, reflected K.C. with amusement. Excellent material for mimicry. The lads at the club were in for a good laugh that evening.

His good mood inflated further; he pushed the protesting gear into position, and the jeep lurched to motion. These communists were a joke! Imagine trying to stir up labour trouble in his Garden!

The jeep bumped over the uneven road, past neat, orderly tea bushes punctuated by the regular upthrust of trees. His Garden. His world. He loved it.

He laughed at the memory of the dhoti-clad Ray gesticulating so ridiculously. Damn fool man, wasting his eloquence on such unresponsive soil.

But Leela, of course, had succumbed to all this ridiculous talk. Absurd. Your paniwalla is rude—so a revolution is in the air. Your ayah gets temperamental—"Didn't I tell you, K.C.! Something's wrong." Women!

He glanced at his watch. He was late. His foot increased its pressure on the accelerator. The jeep bumped with greater violence in an attempt to pick up speed.

In the large gracious bungalow, Leela waited, patient behind the tea trolley. Cigarette smoke curled lazily over her thick short-cropped wavy hair. A discarded *Woman's Own* lay next to her on the overstuffed chintz sofa.

She heard the jeep grind to a stop outside.

"Barua!" she called, "Sahib's home. Bring the tea."

She was halfway through her second cigarette when he came into the drawing room, bathed, refreshed, his slippers flip-flopping on the wooden floor.

"Hullo love!" he kissed her forehead. "What's new on the home front?"

"You'll only laugh if I tell you," she replied.

"Another revolution brewing?" he teased.

"Really K.C. You make a joke of everything. Of course there's no revolution. But all the same there's something wrong. Thing's are just not as they used to be. There used to be a time when there were ten servants to take the place of every one I dismissed. Now I can't get a satisfactory bearer to replace the one I threw out a fortnight ago. Each and every one has been lazy and rude. Barua is doing the cooking and is serving as well, and he is very resentful of the additional burden. He's going to resign any day and that'll really leave us in a mess."

"Don't worry, darling," said K.C., attacking his steaming omelette with relish. "I'll find you a good bearer tomorrow."

"Don't worry! Don't worry! You repeat the phrase as though it were a magic formula. Of course, I worry. I'm the one who'll have to cook and clean and everything if he resigns."

"You'll have your bearer tomorrow, I promise."

Nothing could disturb his good mood. Not even a discontented wife.

It was Friday, the film night at the club. The film was an old, but entertaining, picture. Later, when the men had established themselves at the bar, K.C. launched into his act. The catch phrases, the grossly exaggerated gestures, the additional flourishes invented on the spur of the moment were rendered with a perfect sense of timing. K.C. was a talented mimic. The wooden floor shook as the men stamped and hooted in appreciation. Though he tried to look unaffected, K.C. was enormously pleased. Everyone had roared with laughter, except young Kapur. Damn fool young man. No sense of humour.

Arun Kapur picked up his whiskey and moved over to the ladies.

"May I?" he asked as he pulled up a chair.

There was a chorus of pleased assent. Kapur was a bachelor.

Tea Leaves

The ladies adored him, and mothered him to distraction.

"Your health, Mrs. Sanyal!" He raised his glass towards Leela.

She smiled and inclined her head slightly in acknowledgement.

"Really, K.C. is a scream!" twittered Edna with her archly conspiratorial air. It was an expression she had acquired in her conscious effort to show friendship on an equal footing towards the Indian management personnel. It had been her only concession to Independence.

"I noticed you didn't laugh at my husband's story." Leela liked to throw the boy off balance. It accentuated his little boy lost look.

Arun shifted uncomfortably in his chair.

"It's not that the imitation wasn't funny, ma'am," he explained earnestly. "Your husband is an excellent mimic. It's just that I'm worried, and I find it hard to take the whole affair so lightly. Labour trouble is a funny thing. One minute there's nothing, everything seems fine. The next minute—pfft! Like a conflagration. Impossible to put out."

"So you anticipate labour trouble!" persisted Leela. Arun had a slight American accent. It sounded attractively incongruous in this the last stronghold of the British Raj. Her impossible bracelet jangled as she tipped the cigarette ash into the heavy brass ashtray.

"Ma'am, it's hard to say. My boss obviously doesn't agree with me, and he's the one with all the experience. But all the signs are there. It's all under the surface, ready to erupt. There's violence all over West Bengal. What gives the Doaz its special immunity?"

"I can answer that question, my boy." K.C.'s hand clapped his young assistant on the shoulder. "It's not the Doaz, an inanimate area of land, that is immune. It is the Industry that has breathed life into this land which is immune. It is immune because of the very nature of its existence, its historical identity. Why, we've been in existence for hundreds of years, and have never had any serious labour trouble. This is tea, my boy, not jute . . . or . . . or . . . coal, or some such thing. We are not even a part of the agitated world outside. Why, my labour loves my tea bushes as much as I do. It's something we have created together. Their fathers worked on this land before them, and their fathers' fathers. And it will be their children's privilege to harvest the tender shoots of this same soil. No, my boy. A hundred Rays can talk themselves blue in the face, yet never be able to stir the labour to hostility. I have been here for twenty years. I know."

So, though the crowds gathered and increased day by day, K.C., oblivious, unconcerned, passed by, smiling with indulgent contempt. Let them enjoy this new tamasha while it lasts, was his only reaction.

In the meantime Leela had stopped dismissing bearers. She had discovered that a lazy, rude bearer was better than no bearer at all. Her vague fears persisted. So many little incidents. Yesterday Edna's cook had just got up and left. And all because she told him that the roast was inedible. It was no use telling K.C. He would only laugh and repeat what he always said: "Leela, you are getting to be a tiresome old woman. You get an idea fixed in your head, then look for trivial incidents to lend proof to your theory."

The months passed. K.C., secure in the infallibility of his orderly world, continued his daily rounds, a genial King Canute, oblivious of the canker corroding the innards of his beloved world.

Till the day they drove over to the Thompsons' for dinner. It was a typical tea garden party, relaxed, enjoyable. The same faces, the same talk. From seven-thirty till way past midnight the ice cubes clinked in whiskey glasses. Dinner was finally announced, preparatory to which the ladies went upstairs to powder their noses and the men went outside to water the roses. It was then that K.C. heard about Langhorn.

Langhorn, who had held the tennis trophy two years running, the eccentric widower with two teenage children in a school 'back home' somewhere. Dead. Sickeningly, brutally, murdered.

The men were surprisingly subdued during dinner. The chattering ladies, intent on bread shortage, children's dress patterns, and insolent paniwallas, never noticed. The party broke up soon after.

It was a long drive home. Hypnotised by the crunch, the bump of the car wheels, Leela fell asleep against K.C.'s shoulder.

For the first time in his Garden life K.C. was worried. The gruesome tragedy had shattered his complacency. He had been a blind fool. He had misjudged the situation deplorably. For such a thing to happen to Langhorn! Such a harmless, good-natured soul. My God! It could have been him. It could have been Leela. What a fool he'd been. His eyes were thoughtful slits focused on the uneven expanse of the dirt road illuminated by the car headlights.

Damn these parties. He always drank too much.

Bump, crunch. Identical roads, identical crossroads. Damn these bloody Naxalites. I'll send Leela away to Dehra Doon. Tomorrow. I'll send a telegram to her parents first thing tomorrow morning. And one to Ashok. He'll meet her at Dum Dum and put her on the train to Dehra Doon. What a fool I've been. My God, if anything had happened to her!

The dark figures blocking the road came into sudden focus. He slammed his foot down on the brake. The car lurched to a standstill. Startled to wakefulness, Leela looked up.

"Oh for heavens sake!" she said. "What are those crazy men doing here at this time of the night!"

Figures, dark shadows, emerging from the tea bushes, walking forward into the light. Silent, expressionless.

"What is it, K.C.?" Still only curious. "Find out what they want. Gosh, I was fast asleep."

She, who for months had been repeating the litany "something's wrong," didn't for a moment connect the advancing figures with her vague forbodings of disaster.

But K.C., still shocked by what had happened to Langhorn, was afraid. His mind raced over the possibilities. Don't panic, he told himself. Get Leela out of here somehow.

By now his fear had communicated itself to her.

"K.C.!" Her voice was alarmed. "What's happening? What do they want? Can't you talk to them?"

Talk to them. It might work. It *would* work. There was nothing to fear. This was his labour. He had known them for years. Determined, his confidence flooding back, he opened the car door.

Thud! The door slammed back against him. The spear slid off the dented door and clattered to the ground. Leela screamed.

The figures, ominous, threatening, still silent, pressed forward.

"K.C.!" She clutched his arm. "Drive. Drive quickly." Her eyes were wide, terrified. "Smash through them. Let's get out of here."

Too late.

His training, his instinctive constraint wouldn't let him do it.

"I can't," he said desperately. "If I injure even one of them, we'll never get out of here alive."

Knuckles pressed against her mouth, eyes fixed on the advancing figures, she pressed her body back against the seat. The sound near her window galvanised her to action. She snatched at the handle and rapidly turned up the side window. Meagre protection against the frightening, expressionless faces outside.

"Turn up your window, turn up your window, quick!" she cried.

"If only I could talk to them," he muttered.

"Quick! Quick!" she implored. "Turn up your window, K.C."

Must get out. Must talk to them. He tried his door handle again. It was jammed shut.

The crowd pushed close against the car. There wasn't even a face he could address. Just hard flat bodies, acrid smelling, stifling against the open window.

"K.C.!" she screamed at him. "Turn up your window."

He obeyed mechanically. He felt as vulnerable as though he sat in an eggshell.

He hadn't prayed since he was a child.

"God! God!" he prayed now. "Help me think straight. Help me get Leela out of this alive."

"K.C., do something!" Hysteria was in her voice.

Frighteningly helpless, emasculated in his inadequacy, he was in no condition to face her hysteria.

"Stop it, Leela!" His voice was clipped, brutal. "Control yourself."

Her head snapped back as though he had slapped her. Womanlike, in the midst of her fear, she could only think that he had never spoken to her so harshly.

A low rumbling swelled through the crowd. Spears were raised. Then, with nerve shattering suddenness, the spears began to bang heavily against the fragile tin roof.

The sob caught in her throat as she flung herself in his arms. He held her shivering body tightly. I should have driven straight through them, he thought desperately. Now the car can't move a foot either way. Oh God, why did I brake! I could have got through then. After hearing about poor Langhorn cut to pieces, why did I brake!

The blows rained terrifyingly on the little car. Inside it was an inferno of sound. The pressing crowd was frightening in its controlled violence. The dented roof caved sickeningly above their heads. The rear glass shattered, but held.

It's me they want, he thought desperately. Not her. If he climbed to the back seat, perhaps the rear door would open. He tried to push her away. She clung to him with frenzied strength.

"Leela, let me go. I'll talk to them. Send them away."

"No! No! Don't leave me! Don't leave me!" Terrified, she wedged him tight behind the wheel. It was impossible to move.

The thunderous cacophony of spears shredded her nerve ends. Leela, shivering, cold, was almost insensible in her fear.

Talk to her, comfort her. He tightened his arms around her.

"They won't hurt us. They are only trying to frighten us. Don't be afraid. They won't hurt us. You know these men. They won't hurt us. Had they wanted to, they would have pulled us out and killed us by now. They don't intend to hurt us. They are only trying to frighten us. You'll see. There's nothing to be afraid of. They won't hurt us."

But he didn't believe what he said. He could only think of Langhorn. Langhorn, who had been dragged out of his house and hacked to pieces.

Paralytic helplessness. Think. Think. His mind went round and round the word like a trapped mouse. A blank mind circling round a meaningless word.

And all the time the darkness, the horrible bodies, spears raised—thudding, thudding. Relentless, terrifying.

Crazed with fear, she was nothing but a shivering, witless animal slumped against him.

Keep the fear at bay. Talk. Say something, anything. Capture her attention.

Splinters of glass strewn inside. Headlights smashed long ago. How long? Ten minutes? An hour? Screaming nerve ends and the incessant banging of terror.

Talk, he told himself, talk.

"He has probably coerced them into this. These communists are devilishly clever. Agree with their policies, or they blackmail you into violence. They would never do this willingly."

Talk. He tried to keep his voice calm, normal.

"And to think that this could hapen in my Garden! They will not hurt us. All those crowds gathering every day. Complacent, self-satisfied fool that I am! But there's nothing to be afraid of. Even when they asked for higher wages, started to make their impossible demands. Fool, cursed fool! To believe I could soft talk them out of anything."

You're making no sense. She's not listening.

Bang! Bang! Thud!

Talk. Keep the fear at bay, even if only for a moment.

"Now I see so much that has made trouble inevitable." His mind was concentrating on choosing lucid sentences. Bang! Bang! Bang! "And young Kapur tried to warn me. So many signs. I should have sent you away long ago, but I never suspected, never believed anything could happen." The numbness of his mind began to lift. Just the mechanics of thinking of the next coherent sentence had cut through the fog of terror.

This thudding had been going on for a long time. How long? He looked at his watch. They had left the Thompsons' house at 1:30 a.m. A forty-minute drive till here. Which meant they had been standing in this nightmare for almost an hour. The hope that flashed through him made him giddy. In his blind comforting of Leela he had unknowingly spoken the truth. This was only to frighten them. No killing was intended. This was just a warning. Give the manager a good scare and let him go.

And even as he was groping his way towards hope, the tide pressing against the car seemed to lessen. He listened. The tempo of the blows changed. They were slower, irregular. Out in the darkness the fearsome body had disintegrated, as one by one the dark figures melted into the tea bushes.

A couple of last blows. A spear hurled from the darkness clattering uselessly a yard from the battered car. Silence.

The lifeless body slumped against him had come to life. Immobile, her face still buried against his shoulder, she listened, disbelieving. The rustle of the tea bushes subsided. Only tangible, vibrating silence.

Spasms of shivering, like gusts from a forgotten past. Her body held in rigid control as though any movement may bring back the horror. His hand stroked her hair gently.

"It's over," he said at last. "They've gone."

She looked up then. Carefully scanned the surrounding bushes. Nothing. The familiar shadows of the garden sprawled in eternal tranquility.

Echoing silence. He still held her.

"It's over," he said again. "There's nothing to be afraid of any more."

He held her till the spasms left her body, then put her gently from him. He tried, without much hope of success, to start the car. The battered engine had taken too heavy a punishment. He leaned over and tried her door. It opened. She shivered in the cool night air. His arm went round her again, comforting, reassuring, but now she smiled. A weak, pathetic smile, but a smile. An owl hooted somewhere.

"Where are we?" she said.

"Close to home. We can walk it."

He took her arm. They walked in silence. The battered car stood there, mute testimony to the nightmare they had come through.

A Slit in the Fabric

Solan. The Khalsa Hotel. I feel the fatigue of the tedious journey slipping away under the opiate of hot tea. I sit next to my wonderfully ordinary husband and watch a group of Pahari women, and wonder, as I always do every time I come to Solan, which of them is Arun's wife. And again the question haunts me—What makes a man throw over an enviable five thousand a month job to eke out a meagre subsistence on a bare two acre piece of land? The sins of the father? The mother? Raj Srivastava?

Arun and I were in college together. He had always been oddly reticent about his family. My unabashed curiosity invariably bumped up against the blank wall of his characteristic noncommital shrug. It wasn't till we had known each other for almost two years that he suddenly sprung the matter-of-fact dinner invitation on me.

"I'll pick you up at seven," he said. "We're having dinner with my folks."

I spent the rest of the day in a fever of nervous anticipation. The only reliable information I had about his family was that his father was a brilliant but underpaid economist married to a somewhat less brilliant economist wife.

I had expected a picture book professor's cottage, gay with climbing bouganvillea, its privacy zealously guarded by a shock of heavy foliage, but Arun's motorcycle spluttered up to a large ramshackle bungalow, headlights playing on the dirty green residue of recent rains. Arun strode through the badly lit veranda into an even dimmer hall, and I followed, surprised by the contrasting comfort of the drawing room beyond.

Professor Batra looked sufficiently absent-minded to satisfy my romanticised image of a brilliant professor. His wife was clever faced and rather intense. With them was a colleague and, I guessed, dear friend, introduced to me as Raj Srivastava.

Once the initial introductions and handing of drinks was over, it didn't occur to any of them to pay particular attention to us. We were just an accepted and welcomed part of their environment and they turned to us as and when the conversation permitted, which wasn't very often. I liked that. It left me free to formulate my impressions, free to absorb the charming atmosphere of complete informality, free to wonder why Arun had been so oddly reticent about them.

It was probably my conscious probing of the atmosphere plus my predisposition to sniff out something strange which made me aware of a certain indefinable *something* in the atmosphere. It was something more than that informality which had so enchanted me. It was something more than the unusually deep friendship that obviously existed between the three of them. I found myself listening closely to their spirited discussion on some obscure theory. That there was a shared delight in the intricacies of their subject was evident. But more than the joy in the shared subject was a feeling of positive, uncomplicated enjoyment in the presence of each other. Perhaps it was this unusual naturalness and uncomplicated acceptance of each other that struck me as strange. There was a nebulous but powerful atmosphere of total communication, almost intimacy, which enshrouded the three of them, to the exclusion of everyone else.

And with this half comprehended sharpening of my senses was the growing awareness of Arun's hostility.

Dinner was a brief affair, a necessity of life which was attended to with the minimum amount of fuss or interest. We left soon after. Mrs. Batra invited me, in her uncomplicated friendly manner, to drop in any time I felt so inclined. They were, all three of them, sunnily matter of fact in their goodbyes, neither pleased nor sorry to see us go.

"They're a remarkable threesome," I said as we left.

Arun said nothing, just kicked his motorcycle to throbbing life. Conversation being difficult on a motorcycle, I contained my curiosity till he parked, as he always did, a little away from the hostel gate.

"It was a very enjoyable evening, Arun," I observed, sliding off my perch. "Thank you for taking me. They share a very unusual friendship, those three."

I waited for him to add his comments. I should have known better.

A Slit in the Fabric

"But you know, there's something—something I can't put my finger on, in the atmosphere!" I was tossing out leads, hoping he'd make the right response which would enable me to pry further. But Arun was still staring morosely into space.

"Who's this Raj Srivastava?" I tried a more direct approach. "Is he teaching somewhere?"

"At the Institute."

"So close by? Really Arun. You could at least have introduced him to me earlier. He's such a close family friend. An uncle, almost."

"Yes, almost," he echoed bitterly.

"Why, you don't like him!" I said as though I had just discovered it.

"No," shortly.

"I thought him charming."

No response. I decided to try another angle.

"Your mother doesn't teach, does she?"

"No."

"What does she do all day? I mean, now that you're not home either."

"What she's always done."

"What's that?" Really, this was like pulling his teeth out. He could be so exasperatingly uncommunicative.

"Oh, she sits in the Coffee House, occasionally writes odd newspaper articles." He shrugged his characteristic non-commital shrug.

"You know, I've never seen three people communicate so splendidly. There's such a deep interest in each other's opinions, such a comfortable intimacy between them."

Arun was glowering most forbiddingly. I was beginning to get very suspicious about the Mrs. Batra-Raj Srivastava relationship. My perverse curiosity egged me on.

"How long have you know Raj Srivastava?"

He shrugged again.

"Long enough."

"Where does he live?"

"What the bloody hell is the matter with you!" He turned on me savagely. "How does it concern you? What the hell are you trying to ask? Do you want to know if he and my mother are lovers? Yes they are, damn you!"

I was shocked. He had never spoken to me so harshly. But Arun was like one demented. The carefully secured floodgates of his emotion burst open with shattering force.

"It's the most bloody sick situation in the world. There they are, the three of them, living together happily, with her equally in love with both!"

"You mean your father knows!" I gasped. Her and him, yes. But all three!

"Of course he knows. One can call my mother anything but underhand. She doesn't care enough about anyone to make subterfuge necessary. No, the first thing she did when she decided that she and Raj loved each other was to tell my father. I believe he said something silly like, 'Yes? Nice boy. I knew you'd like him.' It was only when she told him that she planned to shift in with Raj that he became mildly annoyed. After all, how would he ever be able to locate his papers without her. So, since he's an ingenious old bastard, he put forward what seemed to be an ideal solution. Instead of Mother's shifting into Raj's pokey little bachelor apartment, wouldn't it be a better idea for Raj to shift in with them. After all, hadn't Raj been grumbling just the other day that he needed another bookcase but had nowhere to put it? It was a convincing argument, so Raj moved in. Everyone was happy. Except me. So I moved out at the first opportunity."

"Oh Arun!" I said impulsively. "I'm so sorry."

"It makes me sick!" he said violently. "I want to throw up right in the middle of their unruffled lives. Right on them. Make them look disgusted, make them aware of the filth on them, shake them out of their damned selfish unconcern towards the world and values around them."

He was trembling with what I first thought was rage. Then I noticed that his great shoulders heaved to hoarse tearing sobs. I just watched him helplessly, so ashamed of the agony I had unleashed with such frivolous irresponsibility.

"Suppose you try telling her how terribly all this affects you," I ventured softly.

"Telling her? You think I didn't try? I stormed at her and shouted and cursed, and pleaded to her good sense—everything I could think of. She just sat and listened quietly. Then she said in her maddeningly rational voice:

"Son, you can't live my life, just as I can't live yours. You can't use emotion to blackmail me into conforming to your set of principles. I have my own set of principles which may not make much sense to you. Maybe they will one day, maybe they won't. We are both individuals exercising individual sets of choices. How does a situation I make for myself upset or concern you? It does not encroach on your liberties in any way."

"You see what I mean?" His eyes were hurt, pathetic. "There's no way I can approach her. She doesn't try to understand. Her theory is that everyone lives for himself, that there is no such thing as a selfless action, that the very selflessness of an action is giving the doer a certain satisfaction by the very negation it implies. So, naturally, it never occurs to her to consider anybody. When I was a child she played with me when *she* felt like it, not because I needed her. If she sits with father it's because *she* feels like doing so. And he—all this shit seems to make sense to him too. He's another funny character. He was offered a terrific job in the Education Ministry or Finance Ministry or something, but he turned it down. Why? Because he prefers pottering around discussing abstract theories, or drinking interminable cups of china tea, achieving nothing concrete in spite of the great brain and knowledge he is blessed with."

He was quiet for a while. I didn't say anything. I was afraid of distressing him further.

"Look at that damn house they live in. It's just as ramshackle now as it was when they shifted in twenty years ago. They haven't so much as bothered to plant a tree in that disgraceful garden. From moment to moment. That's how they live. I think they're vaguely aware of the existence of a past. They probably discovered it in the History of Economic Theory. But I'll be damned if any of the three are at all aware of the existence of a future.

"How did Raj come into the picture?" Damn my curiosity. I just had to know.

"Colleagues at the Institute. Another one living in the abstract world of theories. But he could afford to. He had no family, no responsibilities, nothing."

That frightening storm of emotion was spent. He brooded darkly and then, for the first time, I think, he acknowledged:

"I suppose it was inevitable that they should be attracted to each other—the three of them. He is another oddball. He went to Cambridge once, to write a thesis. He is an intense kind of chap and he probably poured his blood into that damned thesis. He worked on it for seven months. One night in winter he ran out of coal or whatever it was that he used. So he picked up all his notes and threw them into the fire. Just like that. See what I mean by living only in the present? At that moment he needed the heat, so he picked up the only combustible material he had. And characteristically, he never once regretted the action. The next day, he packed up his bags and returned to India. Said he'd gotten sick of the damn thing. What was he going to do with a thesis anyway!"

He had talked himself into a state of exhaustion. Funny, I never realised that one could actully hear silence. I shifted my weight from one leg to the other. How long had I been standing? He smiled faintly through the pallor of his face. "You make a good listener. Thanks."

He was thanking me! I felt awful. He touched my cheek lightly.

"It's pretty late. Are you sure you'll be able to get in?"

I nodded. My legs had begun to tremble with fatigue. He helped me over the wall. A couple of minutes later I heard his motorcycle splutter to life.

Arun never mentioned his family again. It was as though that night had never existed. We graduated soon after and he landed a good job with an American bank which anchored him to Bombay. In less than a year our letters had dribbled down to short erratic notes.

I lost touch with Arun in the years that followed. The last I heard of him was a chance meeting with a mutual friend. "Did I remember Arun?" he said. "Well, the blighter had tossed away an excellent future with his bank to go and farm a ridiculously small bit of land somewhere near Solan."

That was ten years ago. I never heard of Arun again. I'll probably never meet him, and I'll probably never know what caused that momentary slit in the fabric of his reticence. But every summer I pass through Solan, and every summer the fragment of my past sparks to life and I wonder once again at the strange quirk of fate that prompted my tormented, conventional Arun to make such an incomprehensible choice.

Close To The Earth

It is a beautiful country, my country. Never has nature manifested herself with such abandoned pride, never has the earth borne the traces of passionate love with such splendour. Caressed, repudiated, and loved in turn, my country stands: lushly verdant, heart-breakingly arid, and awesomely majestic. Many-hued is my country, and many-hued are my people. Creamy white, honey skinned, ebony black, and golden brown are my people, and the earth is alive with echoes of their many moods. It echoes their gaiety, their sorrow, their anger, their restraint. Lush green vies with sombre brown, awesome white towers above the rush of blue waters. It is a beautiful country, my country.

And in my country there is a land in which the earth sings with a pride unequalled by any land. It is the land of the five rivers, the land of plenty, the land of a strong and virile people. Hot-blooded, sentimental, simple-hearted people, these people of the land of the Punjab.

This is the story of the most sentimental, the most virile and the most hot-blooded of them all. A man named Sawan Singh. He was a big powerful man, whose fifty-two years sat lightly on his shoulders. His strength was proverbial, as was his generosity. Laughter came to him easily, so did a quick rush of anger. He was proud of his land, proud of his birth, and, most of all, he was proud of his family.

A small family, his. Only two stalwart sons. He had married a gentle, fragile girl in his youth, and had loved her with all the fiery passion that only a hot blooded Punjabi can give. She was the only one who never fell prey to his volatile temper. With her, he was unfailingly gentle and tender, and she returned his passion with unquestioning adoration. Too shy to voice her love, she let her eyes speak for her, and he basked in the adoration of those eyes, becoming increasingly self-confident, dynamic, and successful day by day. She presented him with two sons, then, two years later, she died. He never remarried. Mistresses he had in plenty. He drained the cup of life with enjoyment, like a true connoisseur, but his ardent, sentimental heart could never conceive of enthroning another woman in place of his deeply mourned wife.

Left to him were his sons: a cherished legacy. He brought them up with stern discipline, watered by an abundance of love. Boys to be proud of—broad of shoulder, tall, good-looking—fine strapping lads. Very alike in looks, but totally different in temperament. The younger son, Atma Singh, had his father's flashing eyes, quick temper, a penchant for trouble, and a positive genius for arousing his father's wrath. He revolted early from his father's uncompromising discipline, incurred many a beating, and returned unscathed to the battlefield. Strong willed, like his father, he asserted his untamed, independent spirit at every opportunity. But in spite of frequent clashes the father could not but feel a joy in this son. He seemed to fill the house, this younger son. With his buoyant step, engaging laugh, and easy familiarity, he had an irresistable charm. There was a contagious joyousness about him. He was impetuous, easily ignited, warm, loving and generous.

As a foil to this impetuous brother, was the older son, Ram Singh. Gentle, thoughtful and considerate was this son, and his quiet goodness was the pivot of their home. Fearless, armed with his understanding and sympathy, he used his innate sympathy and understanding as a mediator between the two impassioned hotheads he loved so dearly. But for his gentle, almost imperceptible control, the father and younger son would have caused irreparable injury to each other. He had that rare gift of communication, where just to talk to him was to understand oneself better. He accepted his father's whims and dictates with typical grace. Yielding caused him so little discomfort and gave his father so much satisfaction. Not that he couldn't, on occasion, bend his father's will to his own. He did it with such gentle tack, that the father was scarcely aware of the manipulation. But it was seldom that Ram Singh sought to influence his father, and certainly never for himself did he wield this influence. He did it only to extricate his turbulent brother from his father's wrath or to benefit some worthy petitioner. No one who sought his help left disappointed, no petitioner left unheard. Quiet, self-effacing, he was nevertheless a pillar of strength to his father, who consulted him at every turn. Towards his younger brother, Ram Singh had an almost fatherly love, and watched and protected him with true parental concern. He took his mother's place, this gentle son, and reaped a rich harvest of love from his family.

It came about that Atma Singh, being brilliant, won a scholarship to the Agricultural Institute in the big city. Ram Singh married a quiet, efficient woman, who in time presented him with three children and looked after his father and himself with admirable efficiency.

The house seemed empty without Atma Singh. The shouts of laughter, the heated discussions on irrelevant matters, that turbulence in the atmosphere, was all gone. Even the colourful, volatile father seemed subdued. He had got too used to the constant clash of wills, and deprived of a satisfactory opponent, vented his spleen on the farmhands. The fields rang with his imaginative, vivid abuses, and many a vocabulary was enriched in consequence.

In the evenings, sitting in the stilled silence of the dying day, soothed by the gurgle of his hookah, the sentimental father's eyes would fill with tears when he thought of his younger son, with his bold, flashing eyes, in a far off city. He dreamed of the day his son would return and he and his boys would work together. He had already chosen a girl for his son—a high-spirited beauty, his best friend's daughter. In her he will meet his match, he chuckled to himself agreeably. Besides, she is a strong girl and will give him many children.

And puffing contentedly, he dreamed away the many evenings till his son's return. At last the day dawned, and Atma Singh returned, his new big-city confidence draped about him with elegance. The father's pride knew no bounds as he watched this self-assured stranger alight from the train. Atma Singh touched his father's feet with grave respect, then gravity abandoned, he flung his arms around, first his father, then his brother, hugging them in turn, laughing, jubilant, his eyes shining, his face glowing with all his transparent happiness at being home again. Old friends, relatives, servants, they were all there, crowding around, voicing their joy, being affectionately hugged and punched in turn. The whole crowd rolled, like one large body, homeward, to continue the long-planned, long-awaited celebration. The little township rang with merry-making. The fatted calf was killed. Good food, good wine, had never flowed so freely. Never had men seen such celebration, or witnessed such gaiety. The night vibrated to the intoxicating beat of the bhangra and the men danced till dawn. The wedding date was set, the dowry agreed upon to mutual satisfaction.

The father's cup of joy had overflowed. Then began the clashes. First it was the question of the tractor, then it was the aerial spraying of the crops with insecticide. One disagreement after another. In the fields, in the house, frayed tempers, a total disinclination to compromise; father and son simply could not work together amicably. To begin with, the father willed himself with superhuman forbearance, to listen to his son's new-fangled ideas. But to listen, and to listen only once, was all that he could school himself to do.

The young coxcomb! He wanted to replace the well-tried and so obviously successful methods of his forefathers with some ridiculous, untried, classroom techniques. And not only replace, but replace without any consideration to the cost involved. Twenty thousand rupees for a tractor! And his fields to be sprayed with poison gas. Impossible. This pitiful little spawn of his loins sought to instruct him on the profession he had followed from his infancy. God in heaven. This was too much for his self-acknowledged superhuman patience! In vain did Ram Singh reason, pacify and beseech. In vain did he marshall all his mediating skill. They were both equally tactless. The inevitable happened. Beside himself with anger, Sawan Singh partitioned the land of his forefathers and banished his recalcitrant son from his sight. The marriage celebrations were suspended, the intended bride married another.

In vain did Ram Singh plead.

"Father, he is young. For many years he has been saturated with those ideas so alien to you. Give him understanding. Surely, it was for these very new ideas that you let him be torn away from the family hearth. Surely, it was for this very learning he spent those lonely years in an unfriendly city. Now would you deny him his learning? Would you turn him out for justifying his years of hard work? He is young. Time will sift the impractical ideas and leave him with an ideal synthesis of the old and the new. Give him time. With a little understanding he will inevitably bow to your will.'

"Silence!" thundered the implacable father. "I forbid the mention of his name in my house. He who acknowledges his existence is my enemy. From now on I have only one son."

And so it was that the house fell silent again. The father's terrible wrath lodged in every nook and corner, forbidding disobedience. Atma Singh might never have existed. Except in memory. The father's stubborn pride ignored his wounded heart, and the ignored wound festered to bitterness. True to his word, he never mentioned his son or his bitterly hurt pride, but he never ceased to think of both. Ram Singh, in turn, longed for the sight of the brother he had loved, protected, and reared with such brotherly pride. He loved his volatile young brother no less than he loved his stormy father. He felt heartrendingly torn in two. Habit kept him obedient and ever mindful of his father's wishes, but his heart inspired him to constant effort at mending this tragic breach.

Troubled and distressed, Ram Singh was walking home one evening, and walking home, met his brother. Not to acknowledge him was out of the question. They embraced again and again, and loathe to lose this heavensent opportunity, they went to the nearby cinema together in search of a little privacy.

In a small town can any act remain undetected?

Ram Singh returned to face, for the first time, his father's unreasoned, uncontrolled anger. Ever since he had heard of this act of perfidy, Sawan Singh's blood had been pounding in his head. His hands had been itching to shake his traitorous son like the rat he had proved to be. With redoubled fury he watched Ram Singh approach. Disloyalty, and from this son! What a contemptible hypocrite this son had turned out to be. All that seeming obedience while he betrays me the moment my back is turned. This is how he has repaid my love. Make me the laughing stock of the whole town, will he? I'll show them how I treat a traitor. Die traitor! And with blind, insane rage, the father lifted his kirpan and slashed at the traitor in front of him.

It was the compassion in those dying eyes that jerked him back to sanity. With horror he watched the ebbing life of his favourite son. The enormity of his anguish hit him like a blow, and he knelt. Gently, gently, he cradled his child. His life, his whole future lay in those dimmed eyes, and he watched the light of those eyes fade forever.

It is a hot-blooded land, the land of the Punjab, where anguished remorse stalks silently behind pride, and where a father died that day with his son, leaving an empty shell to walk, talk, and tend the silent fields; an empty shell to live among men, and gaze with unseeing eyes at the beautiful land he had once loved so well.

The Patriot

It is five o'clock in the morning. In another hour they will hang my son. I have watched the night out, fearful of the approaching dawn, but the dawn has come, and coming is the dread hour when my son shall be no more. I tremble on the brink of total despair. But there is time yet, and I believe in miracles.

• • •

My son! My son! Does your resolute courage still hold firm? Do you exult in the passing hours that bring you so close to the fulfillment of your destiny? I watch and pray, and hold firm the courage which you have willed to me. But, oh, the treacherous lump that swells in my throat, and the insistent flood which presses against my eyelids! But it is not time yet. The time to weep is yet to come. My son still lives, and watches the night I watch, marvelling at the beauty of the world, and at the joy of being alive. And I, I live with him, minute by minute, hoarding up each passing splendour, conscious of each moment lost forever.

• • •

And as I sit and watch, the memories crowd about me. It seems like yesterday that I used to watch you coming down the dirt road, bare toes curling against the hot powdery dust, pyjama splattered with the mud of exhuberant play, shoes strung carelessly across an indifferent shoulder. And in absurd contrast I remember the day of your return. Tall, smiling, surely the pride of some Western tailor, your dear skin paled by the English sun. Oh the comfort of your arms, so strong, so secure. Strange, that even now I can smile. Smile with that remembered thrill. Marvel afresh at the unfamiliar length and breadth of you. My son. A man.

How did it start, my son? You never told me, and I didn't ask. There was always so little time. When could I ask?

My son. So light-hearted, so endearingly frivolous. Always laughing, always teasing. If only I could die instead of him.

I can never forget that day.

"Ma, don't delay me with questions. I can't explain anything just now. No time. All I can tell you is that I am a revolutionary wanted by the police. I must go into hiding. Immediately. They will be coming for me now, anytime. Tell them I am out of Lahore somewhere. Tell them anything. For God's sake, Ma. Get a hold on yourself. Don't fail me now. Everything depends on you."

He let me go abruptly. Rushed to the door. Stopped. Came back.

He held me gently, cradled my shocked face against his shoulder. "Mother, dearest Mother! I'm sorry. Truly sorry. It's only for a little while that I must hide. I'll come back. Very soon. I promise. Don't cry. Everything will be allright. I promise."

And like a whirlwind he was off. One minute he was there, and the next minute there was just the stillness of the house to mock my uncomprehending tears.

The police did come, but not till I had managed to dry my bewildered tears. I was suitably cold, disbelieving, and positive of my speedily invented facts. My son had gone to visit my brother in Allahabad in connection with a private family matter. He had left early this morning and I didn't expect him back for a week. They were undoubtedly mistaken in the identity of the man they were looking for. My son, I told them, was above reproach.

But how bitterly my heart ached when they left unconvinced. How could he, I thought to myself; how could he, with his family background, join this group of malcontents gathered from the very dregs of society. What were these revolutionaries but a batch of discontented youngsters? Hadn't the British always treated us with justice? Were our rights and liberties curtailed in any way? What was this illusory cause he had championed with such total disregard to his family name, and in preference to a secure and comfortable future? I could not understand. I could not understand.

I had no news of him for two days. Then on the third day, when I was in the crowded vegetable market, a young man came up behind me and murmured just loud enough for me to hear. "Kumar wants to see you. When I leave, follow me, but try not to do it too obviously."

The Patriot

Hardly daring to look at the strange young man, I obediently sauntered behind him, my heart thudding with anticipation. There was a tonga waiting at the end of the lane. He motioned me into it. I thought he would come with me, but the tonga jerked to motion as soon as I sat down. It was only another ten minutes to our destination. The house in the cluttered street had a bland innocuous facade. A narrow flight of steps led to a small dismal room, and there he was—smiling and unharmed, my son.

My son sat next to me on the dilapidated sofa, and I stroked his hand and tried to hold back the tears.

"Mother!" He smiled gently, compassionately. "Smile at me. That's better. You know you are the most precious thing in my world, and I hate to see you so sad."

I pressed his hand. What could I say?

"Believe me, I have spent many anguished hours of indecision. I have fought against my beliefs, shut my eyes to the humiliation of my people, and have tried so hard to ignore the knowledge of my responsibilities to my country. But my beliefs were too strong and my responsibilities too insistent to be thrust aside."

He got up and began to pace up and down the small room.

"If I could but explain to you how I rage against the injustice of my beautiful, abundantly endowed country yoked to a small island, compelled to pull this puny island to prosperity and progress at the cost of her suffering starving millions."

He turned his agitated face in my direction, gave a short humourless laugh, and said, "You look bewildered, mother, and I am not surprised. I get carried away by the rush of my emotions."

"I don't understand anything any more." I felt so helpless, so *uneducated*. If only his father had been alive! "When you say all this, it sounds very grand, but what is it to us. We have everything."

"Have we? What about that bench I showed you in Mussoorie— 'Dogs and Indians not allowed'. What about all those first class railway compartments labelled 'For Whites Only'. What about our pride—or lack of it. Of course there are affluent people like us who live in comfort and security—and are even bold enough to ride first class. Money, even brown money, is respected everywhere! But we are but a fraction of our country's million. The majority of India lives in primitive darkness, shut out from the rays of education and progress. We are kept dependent on the British for all our needs. We do not even manufacture our own clothing. The best jobs, the best opportunities are reserved for the ruling class. The most intellectual and talented Indian is considered inferior to a mediocre Englishman. We have been drugged into a belief of our own inferiority and accept our humiliation with helpless submission."

His eyes were fierce, unyielding.

"I cannot bear to watch the destruction of a great and good people, I cannot bear to think of the world striding ahead while my once proud country, with her history of splendid achievements, humbly bows her head in submission to a lesser nation. I cannot stand and watch and bear the unnecessary humiliation of it, my mother, and so I must fight. I fight to raise my country from the dust into which she has fallen. I fight to give her back her pride. I fight so that your grandchildren may stand proud and equal in opportunity to any man anywhere in the world."

He was silent, and I was silent too. I understood his intense involvement with his cause, but I still could not understand the cause itself. Parts of what he said made sense to me, but surely there were other ways of bringing these grievances to light. My son was well placed, respected, with access to the best of British society. I had no doubt that my grandchildren would have the same privilege. Why must he take up the cudgel for the faceless millions! Let those who had been wronged fight for themselves.

My son knew me well and could read my thoughts in my eyes. "It is difficult to explain my beliefs within the frames of your references," he continued quietly. "Your world is so limited, for you, my mother, are a typical Hindu woman. It was not thought important for you to read or write, or take an interest in affairs outside your immediate family. As long as your family prospered, you were content. And there are millions like you, my mother. That has been our tragedy. But those of us who think, know. And knowing, must act. Have faith in me, my mother. Though you find me incomprehensible, know that I would not lightly sacrifice your peace of mind. Believe me, I have thought hard before I have taken this step. Your happiness, I know, is in my happiness, and I can never find happiness till I see my country free."

I knew then how fruitless it was to argue. He was totally committed and I knew it. There was nothing for me to do but pray for his safety.

In the beginning he found many opportunities to visit me

The Patriot

unnoticed, but as his reputation grew, his visits became less frequent till they ceased altogether. I had to be content with his letters which sometimes reached me weeks after they had been written. I would carry his letters next to my heart and have them read out to me by our faithful Munshi. I lived for the day he would see the fulfillment of his dreams, and I would at last find the fulfillment of mine.

I think of the normal happy life we could have had, and the day I was ill. So ill and so alone. Weeping and despairing, it seemed I would never know happiness again, and a young girl came to see me. A young girl I had never seen before with a long thick plait of hair swinging at her back, with the glad vivacity of her exhuberant temperament restrained by the compassion in her eyes. There was an engaging lack of self-consciousness about her as she said Namaste.

"My name is Lalita," she told me, "and I have come from your son. He gave me these to deliver to you."

I slipped the soiled and crumpled package, which spoke of days spent in my son's pocket, under my pillow. It was too precious a gift to be shared with a stranger. The letter I could not read, so I handed it back to her asking her to read it to me. As she read the letter, I pictured my son sitting in front of me, laughing and teasing me as he used to do.

My dearly beloved Mother,

I touch your feet in my mind and I fold you to my heart, and as I think of you, my heart smiles at the memory of all the wonderful days gone by. It will not be long before I come home forever, and then I shall eat and sleep and eat and sleep till you scold me for being a no-good idle fellow. I hope you have not been wasting your time in idle tears and have been filling your godown with pickles and chutneys and all those delicious concoctions you make so well. I am going to eat paranthas with mango pickle and curd for every meal, so mind you stock up well. Get to work, woman!

Your very loving, very hungry son.

I was enormously cheered by the letter though I would not admit it.

"My poor son!" I said mournfully. "God knows whether he ever gets enough to eat."

"He certainly wasn't hungry when he wrote the letter!" answered the girl with a laugh. "He had just eaten an enormous meal and had a bowlful of fruit in front of him which, I have no doubt, he consumed later."

I couldn't help but laugh with her. There had been a touch of asperity in her remark, just enough to shake me out of my self pity. She looked very much at home in the big armchair next to my bed, and my heart warmed to the fresh innocence of her face. Her youth brightened the sick room, and I was glad of her company.

"Have you known my son long?" I asked, longing for a glimpse into my son's unknown world.

"Oh no. I have only met him once. He hid at our house for a night. I slipped in behind my father when he went to the godown where your son was hiding. My father was displeased, but he didn't say anything. I just sat in the shadows and listened to them talk. Later my father said goodnight and left, and I would have followed him, but just then your son asked me if I would deliver a gift to you. 'My mother is a very sad and lonely woman,' he told me, 'and it would cheer her up if you went to see her. I love her dearly, and worry about her as much as she worries about me. In fact I would like to write a letter to her if you could bring me some paper and a pen.' I brought him the paper and sat with him while he wrote the letter."

She blushed, then quickly added, "And so here I am."

I noticed the blush and smiled inwardly. So there was more to the story, I thought to myself. It was obvious that my son had charmed her too. But she seemed a good girl, and I was glad. Perhaps she would be the force that would bind my son to domesticity.

"Tell me about yourself," I said, probing gently for information about her family. "Do you have any brothers and sisters?"

She told me all about herself, her father, and her family, with naive unsuspecting simplicity. I could not have chosen a better family had I arranged my son's marriage myself.

"Come and see me often, child," I said. "You dispel my despondency with your lively presence and make me believe that happiness is drawing close at last."

After that she came to see me often, and I talked to her of my son. Memory after memory I recounted to her, delighted to have such an interested audience. The more I grew to love her, the more I hoped that we would live together one day, the three of us, in a house alive with the patter of childish feet and childish laughter. I said so to her one day and she blushed painfully as her eyes filled with tears, and I knew that she hoped as I hoped, and I loved her all the more.

Kumar's letter were always filled with such cheerful optimism that I was unprepared for the shattering suddenness of the blow when it fell. Even when they told me of my son's arrest I did not see my future crashing about me.

No, they had not caught him, they said. He had surrendered himself to the police.

Why should he surrender himself to the police, I asked myself. Why? Obviously he must have some plan in mind, and, I thought foolishly, will of course escape at will. At least now I knew where he was and could go and visit him. It has been a year since I last saw him . . .

Strange, how it never occurred to me to be anxious. The legends that had grown up about him had reached even my ears. It was said that he had once walked into a police station, given false information regarding his own whereabouts, drunk tea with the constable in charge, and walked out unmolested.

The jail authorities were very courteous and let me go in to him immediately. I went in with happy anticipation, armed with the fruit and sweetmeats I had hastily put together.

My heart almost stopped when I saw him. This reed, thin stranger with the haunted sunken eyes, was this my son? Was all that challenging vitality sacrificed at the altar of his nebulous ideals? Oh my son, how heartbreaking the change.

And as he embraced me, I held on to him for a long time, not trusting myself to look at his ravaged face. I think he wept a little too, though by the time I looked up his eyes were dry again.

I smiled wet-eyed, and said tremulously, "You need a mother to look after you See how thin you've become!"

"Don't let's talk about me yet, mother. First tell me all about yourself and all about that precious world I stepped out of so long ago."

I sat beside him on the matting spread on the prison floor and answered all the questions that welled out of his memories of a lost world. Friends, relatives, servants, he inquired about them all, and at last he came to the question I knew he had wanted to ask from the start.

"And what about Lalita. Does she visit you often?"

"Yes, my son. She comes often and I have grown to love her like a daughter. She has become a part of my dreams of our future."

"There can never be a future," he said tiredly.

"Why? Don't you care for her? I know you write to her, and I know she cares for you. Cares for you very deeply."

His shoulders sagged a little as I said this, and his face was heavy with unhappy remorse.

"I should never have involved her in a friendship which was doomed to end in tragedy," he murmured to himself. Then to me he said with such intensity, "I never meant it to end like this, mother. I was young and optimistic and invulnerable. I was the one destined to taste the heady flavour of victory. She was so beautiful when I first saw her, lingering in the dark shadows, gazing at me with so much open admiration. I would have been more than merely a man had I been unaffected by the fresh loveliness of her. I had to talk to her, had to establish some sort of contact I could later build on. I talked to her that night as though she were my oldest, dearest friend, and I carried the memory of her like a torch to dispel my moments of unhappy uncertainty. I knew I would marry her if I came out of this alive, but fate has willed otherwise."

"What do you mean, my son? Why should fate have willed otherwise. You have done enough for your country. Now is the time to give up all this foolishness and settle down. How much more can you do! Look what you've done to yourself! I don't know what impossible tortures you must have subjected your body to, to have worn it down to such a shred!"

He smiled at my indignation and said, "No impossible tortures, mother. My body just couldn't live up to the fire that burnt within me. Even now it is only this traitorous bulk of matter which has let me down. My spirit still rages unconsumed. You see, mother, the game I played required more than courage. It was a game of nerves."

And as he talked, a picture began to form, of a man hunted to the point of exhaustion, suspicious of his friends, always on the look out for his enemies, ever watchful of the inevitable betrayal.

"You run and you hide, and then run and hide again, in an unending sequence of monotony. So preoccupied do you get with this fight for survival that you can think of nothing else. You see betrayal in every face, bury your fatigue under fitful, ever-watchful sleep, and know that there can never be any respite for you, not for a long, long time. I ran till I could run no more. I was exhausted and useless, and I knew it. There was one last service I could render my cause—a public trial and a public execution. Mother, my mother, be brave and look at your son with pride. We were chosen, you and I, for the glory of our country. My role is easier. To you must fall the burden. It is your sacrifice that will lift your country high. High among the greatest nations of the world. It is your sorrow that will be the solace of the stricken millions, crushed, demoralised, and hopeless, and will gift to them a new found pride, an identity and equality in the world of men. You were made for greatness, mother. Alone, unsung, your sacrifice will change the course of history."

Fine, stirring words. Empty words. What cared I for the millions who lived in torment. I only wanted the life of my son. The lump in my throat swelled and I could hardly speak. I wanted so much to be the mother he expected me to be. Now, at the end of his life, he must not be disappointed. I must rise to the impossible heights he expected. Illiterate, uneducated, I knew instinctively that in my courage was his courage in this last enormous task he had set himself. What was this thing, this Freedom, that he loved so much, that demanded so much sacrifice.

"How do you know," I managed to say at last, "that your trial will end unfavourably?"

"Not unfavourably, mother. It is favourable to our cause if I am condemned to death. Public sympathy will ignite instantly. The trial is bound to end as I expect it to. I have made too much of a following for them to let me go. There is no way out for them. They must execute me. It is inevitable."

His prediction proved to be true. The trial was a mockery. My son was magnificent. His sunken eyes flashed with recaptured brilliance, his proud carriage seemed to fill the dark courtroom with the justice of his cause. I understood little of what he said, but I saw the shamed expressions of the jury, and I understood that the judge passed the sentence he had to pass. The trial, the prosecution, the defence, and the sentence, had all been decided beforehand. This was only the staging of a well rehearsed plot.

Half demented I pushed my way through every hopeful door, knocked my head against every insurmountable wall, and explored every conceivable avenue of escape. All to no avail. The fatal sentence had to be rushed to its conclusion before the people could organise themselves into an effective demonstration.

Now, helpless against the torrent of destiny, I wait and pray. I pray for courage. Courage for him, courage for me. I start at every soft sound outside my door as irrational hope surges through me. It is not time yet. Can this mean a reprieve for my son? Is it my son waiting on the cold doorstep, released to a secure and happy future?

My son! My son! You were made for greatness, but I am but a frail mother, and the weight of so much grief is hard to bear.

The Coloured Bangles

The wooden gate still hung slightly askew. Asha opened it without difficulty, but couldn't quite shut it again. Shutting the gate had always been a problem, and she had always been lectured on the damage done to the vegetable garden by the cows that wandered in. She was surprised at the nostalgia that wafted over her. Now that she didn't belong to the house, hadn't belonged to the house, for so many years, she no longer felt an outsider.

The neem tree spread lush and shady over the cemented pathway. All the vendors in turn had spread their wares under the shade of the neem. Memories of gay glass bangles, of the wooden crank creaking as it extracted fresh sugar cane juice, the smell of freshly roasted peanuts; memories of laughter and jostling, and the smiling eyes of Suresh.

Old Sudama sat by the side of the porch. Not on the wooden bench, but squatting on the ground beside it.

"Are vah! Vah!" he exclaimed, rising with some difficulty. "It's our Bahuji! How many years has it been since these old eyes have seen you?"

"Too many, Sudama. How are you?"

"Put out to pasture," he chuckled. "No more 'Sudama, wash the dishes, Sudama, polish the silver'! No indeed. Now I just smoke my hookah and announce the visitors. How happy they will all be to see you, Bahuji!"

Asha doubted that, but didn't contradict him.

"Tell me, Sudama, does Buaji still occupy the same room she used to?"

"Yes indeed, Bahuji. The same old room. Nothing changes here. Many more children, many more daughters-in-law, but everything remains the same." He suddenly sighed heavily. "Only

Suresh Babu is dead, and you have gone back to your parents."

There was nothing to say to that. She stood irresolute for a moment, then turned and went indoors.

She didn't remember the house being so gloomy and damp, and walked quickly through the otherwise unchanged rooms. The murmur of voices from Tayi's room stopped her. On an impulse she turned and went in.

Three of Suresh's aunts reclined against bolster pillows on the carpet covered by a white sheeted carpet. A baby slept undisturbed on the divan.

"Why, it's Asha!" exclaimed the youngest Chachee. "Come on in, child. Don't just stand there."

Asha went in smiling, bent slightly, hand outstretched, not quite touching Tayi's feet, but making a hopefully adequate gesture. Tayi raised her hand in a vague blessing, her eyes lighting disapprovingly on the heavy twist of gold round Asha's wrist.

"That's a very pretty gold kara," she said pointedly.

Asha flushed, but kept quiet. Her parents were emancipated enough to disregard the old taboos placed on widows, thank God.

She bent in an even more perfunctory gesture over the Eldest Chachee's feet.

"What's the matter?" said the Eldest Chachee tartly. "Do your parents prevent you from properly touching the feet of your elders?"

"She's just feeling irritable today," whispered the youngest Chachee as Asha bent over her. Asha kissed the youngest Chachee with some affection and sat down beside her, leaning back against the familiar uncomfortable contours of the ornate chair pushed back against the wall.

"Come and sit beside me, Bahu," said Tayi peremptorily. She was inflexibly traditional and had always addressed Asha by her title of "daughter-in-law". Asha obediently got up and re-settled herself beside Tayi. "How are your parents, and your brothers?"

Asha went through the routine, tradition-dictated dialogue. The youngest Chachee handed her a glass of chilled sherbet.

"And what brings you here today?" Asked the Eldest Chachee. "Not that we're not delighted to see you," she added insincerely.

"I heard that Buaji was very ill."

"Yes," sighed the Eldest Chachee. "She's been dying for years. I think this time she might even succeed. Not that that's any reason for

The Coloured Bangles

you to come. I thought you two hated each other."

"Suresh loved her," explained Asha somewhat lamely.

"Naturally. She brought him up. She doted on him, foolish old woman, and never forgave you for taking him away."

"I never took him away," said Asha defensively. "We lived here. All those years."

"Ah, but she had to share him with you. What was worse, he loved you."

"What a foolish conversation," snapped Tayi. "Tell me, Bahu, what is your new sister-in-law like? I mean your sister-in-law to be."

"Yes," put in the youngest Chachee. "I hear your brother has just got engaged."

"Yes, to a lovely girl. Not only lovely looking, but very sweet-natured. She looked truly beautiful at the engagement."

"Oh? You mean you were there? At the ceremony?" asked Tayi in disbelief.

Asha coloured faintly.

"Yes."

"Extraordinary," commented the Eldest Chachee.

"My parents do not believe that a widow is inauspicious," said Asha with some spirit.

"Of course not," murmured the youngest Chachee soothingly.

"Bahu," put in Tayi firmly, "their believing or not believing is of no relevance. Their love for you might blind them to the possibility of future disaster, but you should have known better. A belief that has held good for a thousand years, down through a thousand wise elders, must have some truth in it.

"It is a cruel and senseless belief," said Asha passionately. "A widow is a woman like any other. Neither auspicious nor inauspicious. I'm glad I don't live here. You would have relegated me to a slow death the same way you pushed Buaji into the dark, ignored alleyways of life."

"Don't be insolent, Asha," the Eldest Chachee's voice was quelling. "Nobody pushed Buaji anywhere. But she was a wise woman and knew her position."

"Knew her position? She was born into that terrible position," Asha's voice shook with emotion. "She was just a baby when her father carried her round the marriage fire on a silver thali. Her groom was a little boy of five who should have been in bed many hours earlier. By the time she was three years old, she was already a widow, without knowing what the word meant, without ever having seen her child husband. It was criminal."

"Hush, Asha," put in the youngest Chachee seeing the telltale tightening of Tayi's lips. But Asha was long past being silenced.

"I've heard the story. In fact, you are the one who told me, Tayi. About the time when all the children were discussing their new clothes and she went running up to her mother to ask for a green *lehnga* to wear to the *mela,* and her mother said 'But you can't go to the *mela*—you are a widow. And you can never wear colours because a widow must always wear white'. She was only six. She learnt her first cruel lessons at the age of six. She was to learn many cruel lessons in the years to come. How a widow is inauspicious, must never take part in any family festivity or gaiety, must never wear jewellry or ornaments, how a widow is only permitted to look longingly at the wonderful collection of glass bangles the vendor brought to the house every week, and how she must always live in apology for being alive. You never even permitted her to attend Suresh's wedding. She was the only mother he ever knew!"

The baby on the divan began to cry fretfully. The youngest Chachee picked it up and cradled it to sleep. Tayi maintained an ominous silence. The eldest Chachee commented brightly.

"Well, that's very touchingly told. And here I always thought you two hated each other!"

"I was young and thoughtless," said Asha, a little ashamed of her outburst.

"I think you should come back and live with her," said the Eldest Chachee with some asperity. "Then you might remember what a cranky, sour old woman she really is."

"Well," said Asha standing up, her smile a little forced, "I must go and see Buaji. So if you'll excuse me . . . "

Above the soft rustle of her starched cotton sari, Tayi's comment carried clearly.

"She was always a strange girl."

She quickened her step toward Buaji's room. A wire netting door overlooking the courtyard framed the group of children crouched, tense with excitement, round the portly Middle Chacha who was a little plumper, a little balder. Children and Chacha, absorbed in the intricacies of the game he outlined, were quite

The Coloured Bangles

oblivious to the scolding voice of the Middle Chachee. Again she smiled faintly. It had always been so.

Buaji's room was dark and airless. A maid servant rose from the floor near the bed as Asha entered. Buaji, a slight, shapeless mound under the white sheet, didn't stir. Asha looked round for a chair. The maid servant pulled one up to the bed, then silently left the room.

Buaji was awake. Her eyes had turned fleetingly towards Asha before returning to stare at the ceiling fan which slowly stirred the tepid air.

Asha leaned forward and said softly, "Buaji, it is I, Asha."

The eyes continued to look up at the ceiling. The silence in the airless room was intensified by the intruding sounds of outside life: the droned twanging of cotton wool fluffed through vibrating wires, the distant voices of children playing, the brisk swish of a coconut-stem broom.

"I'm sorry I haven't been to see you for so many years."

Again the silence.

"Most of all I'm sorry that you never liked me."

The silence was pointed, eloquent.

"Perhaps it was because Suresh and I met in college and fell in love, because the right to select your own daughter-in-law was denied you. Perhaps I was just too much of an alien—a forward creature with strange ideas."

The eyes remained expressionless.

"Two possessive women, hating to share the man they loved. Well we lost him, both you and I. You lost your son; I lost my husband."

The eyes glowered forbiddingly.

"I've thought about you and me a lot these last few months," went on Asha resolutely. "Both widows, but living in different times. Sometimes I get this strange sense of interchange, my being you, widowed when you were widowed, forced to live out my widowhood 70 years ago. I understand so much I never understood before."

The eyes remained implacable.

"I've brought you a present." Asha opened her cavernous handbag. Paper rustled as she unwrapped her gift. Even in the dim room the brightly coloured glass bangles glowed with a joyous life of their own.

"Times have changed, Buaji. Widows are no longer creatures

set apart, creatures to be pitied, even to be avoided. Today you and I are women like every other woman. A part of the vibrancy of life. It is too late for me to prove to you what a joy life can be. But I've bought you these. They're for you. Today widows can wear anything, go anywhere . . . "

There was nothing left to say. She stood up abruptly, thrust the glass bangles into Buaji's supine hand, and hurried out of the room.

She didn't see the fingers curl lovingly round the smooth contours of the bangles. Nor did she see the tear caught in the furrows of the aged cheek.

Outside, the noon shadows were sharp with contrast. She pressed ten rupees into the grateful Sudama's hand. He hurried after her with his curious lope, securing the slated gate firmly behind her retreating figure. Her high heels sank into the powdery dust as she walked slowly to the bus stop. A car eased up beside her. At the wheel, Ashok looked smug, his eyes dancing at the delighted recognition on her face.

"I told you I'd never lose sight of you. I'm so enamoured of you that I'll even share my car with you. I'll even buy you lunch, maybe even dinner. Maybe never let you go!"

Sudama watched the laughing young woman climb into the car. Round the corner the vendor with the wonderfully coloured glass bangles sauntered leisurely, outside of time, towards the old house, to spread his sparkling collection under the shade of the old neem tree.